To Joy (signature)

DETECTIVE'S APPRENTICE

By

Dewey Richards

Other books by A Dewey Richards MD
SOLUTIONS a Medical Mystery novel
DETECTIVE'S APPRENTICE a sequel
WIDE SWATH a Maine family 1900-1950
LIVE LIVELY LONGER a doctor's RX
JUST MY LUCK, my autobiography
All are available from AMAZON.com
or from the author at adr1996@aol.com

ISBN: 1-4107-6097-9 (e-book)
ISBN: 1-4107-6096-0 (Paperback)
ISBN: 1-4107-6095-2 (Dust Jacket)

Library of Congress Control Number: 2003093719

This book is printed on acid free paper.

Printed in the United States of America
Bloomington, IN

1stBooks - rev. 05/20/03

CHARACTERS NAMED AND DESCRIBED

Doc, Albert Williams, M. D., general practitioner, large man, muscular, wears freshly laundered short-sleeved white shirt, chino trousers, bow tie and pocket protector full of pens.

Zelda Green Gardiner; red hair, very intelligent, twenty-two years old.

Matilda Campbell Parker; widow 25 years, 50 years old, 120 lbs, 5'8" tall, light-brown hair, athletic, attractive, medical office manger, RN & RT, confidant of Doc, bright, good knowledge of human nature, maintains law library, skiing friend of Sgt. Darling, tournament bridge player with David McBee.

Harry Darling; "Handsome Harry", Maine State Police Sergeant, loves Matilda, large man, athletic, good skier, compassionate, honest.

Hiram Murphy; Detective, tough, well muscled, 5'10" tall, loud voice, bright blue eyes, multiple injuries, weak left arm and left leg, quotes proverbs and similes, Harvard graduate, lives like a hermit.

Gloria Ingraham, Maine State Health Nurse, "the State Lady", grossly obese, insensitive, vindictive, aggressive, determined, man-hater

David McBee;	Pharmacist, tournament bridge player, Matilda's lover
Dr. Saul Galliano;	Surgeon with Parkinson's disease
Dr. Franklin Price;	Philandering Surgeon, died with gunshot wound
Sheriff Darcy;	Greenville Sheriff, abrupt, no-nonsense
Mrs. Price;	Petite, widow, gracious, naive
Florence Gifford	Dr. Galliano/Price's office manager, middle aged
Deputy Sheriff	Talkative, incompetent police officer
Butler	Large, muscular, "butler", medical aide to Dr. Galliano
Richard Calzoni	Wealthy, large, mean, vindictive, police benefactor
Virginia Calzoni	Heiress, gracious, large woman
Betsy Lodge	Virginia's Granddaughter, dogs injured, scarred face
Beaches	Editors and owners of Lakewood News
Paul Bryan	Bow hunter, former patient of Doc, student
Elmer Morgan	Caretaker of Calzoni Estate
Ethelyn Morgan	Elmer's wife, housekeeper for the Calzonis
Audie Grant	Trenton Police Officer
Nancy Lodge	Betsy's mother, Virginia Calzoni's daughter

PROLOGUE

The first cold wave of 1972 reached New Jersey, causing near freezing temperatures in the late November afternoon. The Fifth Precinct desk sergeant saw the dapper detective walk in and called out, "Hymie, the commissioner wants to see you. He's in the captain's office."

Hiram Murphy waved and continued walking to the squad room. He hung his topcoat in his locker, nodded to another detective pecking at a typewriter, then took two stairs at time going up to the captain's office on the second floor. The captain's door was open, so Hiram walked in and smiled, "Hi Commish, you wanted to see me?"

The tall thin commissioner stood and shook Hymie's hand. He glanced at the portly captain behind the desk and said, "Hiram, we're both worried about your safety. Have you thought any more about the fed's offer to relocate you with a different identity?"

"Yeah. I thought about it. I like what I'm doing. The mob bosses are all behind bars. It'll take a long time for the syndicate to get reorganized. I think we did them in."

"We're not so sure. There are still some very dangerous characters around. I heard Junior Carrillo is getting the old gang together. He won't be happy that you put his father behind bars."

Hiram laughed, "He's happier than you think. His father kept him under his thumb for years. Now he can do what he wants. He's using the family capital to set up legitimate businesses. I spent a lot of time with him while I was undercover. We're good friends. I'm meeting him at the gym in a half hour to play racket ball. He's a good athlete and very competitive."

The captain spoke up, "I told the commissioner the witness protection is up to you. I think you're being foolhardy, but you know those people better than anyone else on the force. The offer to relocate stands, if you want it."

"Thanks. Thanks to both of you. I'll continue working here. I'll let you know if I feel threatened. If there's nothing else, I'll keep my racket ball date."

The commissioner put his hand on Hiram's shoulder and said, "If you ever need anything, just ask. You did one hell of a job."

Hiram smiled, then stepped away and said, "That's what I get paid for. I'll let you know if I see any part of the mob reorganizing. Junior will know what's going on. I'll ask him this evening."

Hiram got his topcoat and gym bag from his locker and waved to the two officers in the squad room. The gym bag was heavy with the two five-pound barbell weights he was bringing home, but it was only two blocks to the gym, so he started walking briskly to get warmed up for his match. As he approached the entrance, a man stepped out of a car across the street, lifted a submachine gun, and fired a burst at him. Hiram fell, clutching his gym bag to his chest, but the submachine gun kept firing until the magazine was empty. The big man walked over and looked at the riddled body, then trotted back to the car and sped away.

Two patrolmen entering the precinct house heard the shooting. They drew their guns and ran to find Hiram bleeding and unconscious. One stayed with the body while the other called an ambulance. Even though it was too late to do anything for Hiram, they rushed him to the Trenton General Hospital.

TABLE OF CONTENTS

CHAPTER ONE

Matilda's Problem

As the last patient of the afternoon walked to the receptionist desk, Doctor Albert Williams stretched his shoulders back and relaxed. He started to think about his hospitalized patients when he heard Matilda's contralto voice coming from his business office. Eager to see her again, he walked back and stood in the doorway as she continued, "I'm up the creek without a paddle, Zelda. I don't know what to do."

Doc admired the tall athletic woman who had helped him so much. Matilda's figure was impressive in a woman fifty years old. Obviously, she was continuing her vigorous morning workouts. During the ten years she managed his general practice, he came to appreciate her quick mind and analytic ability. The strain in her voice revealed her distress and caused him to wrinkle his brow. Matilda continued her lament to Zelda, the young woman she trained to take her place as Doc's secretary and office manager, "All that time and effort wasted, going off half-cocked. I don't know what I was thinking. What a dunce I am."

Zelda shook her head as she listened, and then noticed Doc, glanced at him and said, "Matilda, tell Doc. He may have some ideas."

Matilda turned and gave him a wry smile, "Hi, Doc. I don't think you can help me this time. It looks like the bed I made for myself isn't a place I can sleep comfortably."

Doc smiled back, "It's good to see you, Matilda. Why don't you both come into my office and tell me about it.

1

The three of us should be able to sort things out. We've done it before."

After the last patient of the day left the office, the group frequently sat and discussed any problems concerning Doc. These informal meetings, initiated by Matilda shortly after Doc started his practice, included Zelda after she joined the staff. All three enjoyed their discussions, and Doc found the information and insight invaluable. Matilda grew up in Lakewood and knew all the family history and the personalities involved, including some relationships that weren't common knowledge. Zelda's keen intellect and common sense helped the other two separate the wheat from the chaff. The discussion helped Doc understand some difficult situations, allowing him to provide the best care for the people of Lakewood, the small town in western Maine where he had his busy family practice.

Doc was an unlikely looking physician, a large boned man with close-cropped hair, built like a professional wrestler. He tried to provide a professional look with his habitual attire of freshly laundered chino trousers, starched short-sleeved white shirt, clipped-on paisley bow tie, and a pocket protector filled with pens. Actually, his soft brown eyes and gentle manner put his patients at ease.

Ten years ago, when Doc bought the house, office and practice from Doctor Chesapeake, Matilda had everything well organized. At the urging of the retiring doctor, she agreed to stay until Doc became established. Matilda ran the practice, functioning as office nurse, x-ray technician, medical assistant and office manager. Independently wealthy after the death of her parents, she planned to become a detective, but delayed her plans when the older physician talked her into helping him set up his practice. He continued to need her assistance, so she kept her plans in abeyance until that doctor retired. When Doc took over the practice, she agreed to stay on a few weeks to get him started. The weeks turned into months, and then into nearly ten years. Finally, she found a way to reach her goal by carefully grooming Zelda to take her place. Matilda had no family responsibilities. Her brief marriage ended with her husband's death in the last days of the World War II. She enjoyed the company of men, but vowed nothing was going to interfere with her plans to become a detective. After spending the last two years training Zelda to give Doc the support he needed, she resigned to follow her dream.

Doc and Matilda first knew Zelda as a pregnant thirteen-year-old patient, deeply depressed and without any family support. With Doc's continuing care and Matilda's friendship and guidance, Zelda matured into an impressive young woman. Her father prevented her from going to high school, but she read voraciously, studying the texts she might have used in school, and then reading associated materials. Her keen mind absorbed and assimilated a wide range of subjects. Matilda and Zelda became close friends. Their personalities and inquiring minds complimented each other. Zelda hoped to attend college, but Matilda persuaded her to postpone her plans and assume the position of office manager for Doc. This left Matilda feeling a little guilty but allowed her to follow her dream of becoming a detective.

The three friends assembled in Docs office. Doc poured coffee for them from his preferred old percolator, then poured himself the tenth cup of the day. He tipped back in his worn brown leather chair, waiting to hear more about Matilda's new career as a detective. For ten years, she gave him support whenever he needed it. Now maybe he could return the favor. The women sat in Doc's worn leather chairs and sipped the strong coffee as Matilda started her story, "I hope you can help me, Doc. If you have time, I'll start at the beginning, the way you like it. Then you'll understand why I'm so upset."

He nodded, took another swallow of coffee and leaned back in his swivel chair. Matilda was usually decisive and self sufficient, but now she looked grim as he asked, "OK. You were eager to get started as a detective when you left here two months ago. Tell us what happened"

"Well, first I made my front parlor into an office. I had a new carpet installed, painted the room warm rose and hung new striped draperies. In Portland, I bought a big desk similar to yours, only in birds-eye maple with a glass top. I bought a green leather swivel chair for me and two matching green leather chairs for clients. My office is set up just like the one you have here."

Doc said, "That must have cost a pretty penny. You are serious about this."

Zelda chimed in, "She's talked about being a detective ever since I met her, Doc. I took her place so she could do it. Now her plans are all wasted, unless you can think of some way to help. Tell him, Matilda."

Matilda glanced from one to the other, then continued, "OK. But let me lay out all the facts, first. I finished my office with a new typewriter, matching maple file cabinets, and a glass front bookcase. The front door opens into the front hall, so I have a separate entrance for my office. I moved a couple of my wing backed chairs and a side table into the hall, so I even have a waiting area."

Doc listened, thinking that Matilda always had good taste. He said, "That sounds like a great start. You should be able to impress your clients in that office."

Matilda continued, "That part is all right. I wrote an ad to go in the paper, and planned to hang out my shingle the next week, but David McBee called to remind me that we'd booked a room together at the Alameda Plaza in Kansas City for the fall meeting of the NACBL, the North American Contract Bridge League Championships. He had the plane tickets, and expected to pick me up the next morning. Dumb me! I'd been so involved in planning for my new career that I'd forgotten our trip to the NACBL games. For five years, we've been partners in the spring and fall championship games, and do quite well in national competition. He's great company, and I did promise I'd go, so I decided opening the office could wait a week."

"So, did you and the pharmacist lose, or were there personal problems there?"

"No, we won a lot of gold points and even got a trophy. We use the Precision bidding system and do very well. It was an enjoyable week. David is an excellent partner in every way. We can spend a week together without him getting possessive and talking marriage."

Doc asked, "You mentioned Precision bidding. What is that? I just bid by the seat of my pants when I play bridge."

"It's a complex system devised by the Chinese for international play. It's not useful for party bridge. I'll tell you about it sometime."

Doc nodded and smiled as he thought about Matilda and David enjoying each other's company, but noticed Matilda's concerned look and asked, "So what's the problem?"

"I'm getting to it. When we got back, I ordered a sign built, wrote ads for the *Downeast* and *New England* magazines, and was digging a hole for the signpost on the front lawn when a State Police car pulled up. My good friend and skiing partner, Sgt. Harry Darling, jumped out of his cruiser. Handsome Harry walked up to me with his big chest pushed out and his stern policeman look on his face. He was obviously upset about something. When I started to give him a hug, he pulled away, and told me the Lakewood News reported the success David and I had at Kansas City. He was green-eyed jealous. He thinks he owns me because we go on ski trips together. I tried to placate him, because he really is one of my dearest friends, and I know he really loves me. After he calmed down, he told me there was early snow at Park City, Utah. He said he wanted to spend more time with me and asked me to spend a ski week with him. I told him I was tied up, but he knew I wasn't working for you any more, and wouldn't take "no" for an answer. To patch things up, I agreed. We had an excellent week of powder skiing."

"So far you haven't described anything but social problems. Is Handsome Harry still upset? I can talk with him."

"No, he'll be fine until I go to another bridge tournament. He wants me to limit my love life to just him, but I enjoy the variety. It's my career as a detective that concerns me."

Doc said, "OK, I guess I have enough background. It sounds like you're ready to roll. So, what's the problem, Madam Gumshoe?"

Matilda became more serious, "Coming home on the plane, Harry asked what I was planting in my front yard. I told him about the sign and finalizing my plans to open a detective agency. Every time I mention becoming a detective, he tries to discourage me. This time he laughed, and said 'You should read your law books. Private investigators have to be licensed. Practicing without a license will get you arrested, and I'll be obligated to do it.' He suggested I plan on a wedding instead of a career."

"He'd like that, but did you find out what it takes to get a license?"

"That's the problem. I thought I just had to apply and register with the state. Harry said I had to get a degree in Criminal Justice, or get experience as a law enforcement officer. I thought getting a license was a simple formality, but I looked it up in the law books my father left me, and he's right. I read the law, and there is one other way. An apprentice to a licensed Private Investigator can apply and take the test after one year. That would be the quickest way, but I'd rather stay in Lakewood. I don't want to move away from my house, and there's no Private Investigator listed in the local phone book."

Zelda spoke quietly, "You see, Doc. There's no way she can do it without leaving Lakewood or going back to school for a couple years. I suggested that she come back and work here, be office manager again, and let me go to college. Then she could help you investigate the medical examiner cases, the unattended deaths. She could do that detective work without needing a license."

. Matilda frowned and shook her head as Doc thought for a moment, then said, "We'd both like that, but there may be another way. I think Hiram Murphy has a private investigator license. When I saw him last month, he said he was working on a couple cases. He worked as a Trenton,

New Jersey police detective until he was nearly killed in a gunfight. Hiram grew up in Maine and returned here to recuperate in the old log cabin his grandfather built. I saw him several times on house calls. When he felt well enough, he took the Maine Private Investigator test and became licensed in Maine. He has a good disability pension from New Jersey, but does a little work as private investigator. He might take on an apprentice for a year. It would get you started and give you some experience. After a year, you could take the test for a license of your own."

Matilda brightened, "That sounds great. How do I find him?"

Doc smiled and held up his hand, "Not so fast. I should explain, Hiram's an odd character who sometimes talks in riddles. He knows his stuff, but you'll have to approach him carefully. He's crusty, even crude sometimes, and acts paranoid, restless, jumps at shadows. Paranoia is not unusual in a person who has a near-death experience, but his is extreme. He has his log cabin fixed up like a fort, and keeps to himself. He posted big "Private Road" and 'No Trespassing" signs at the bottom of the hill. If hunters or hikers drive up his road as far as his cabin, he meets them with a loaded rifle and drives them away. I think I'm the only person who really knows him. Hiram lives like a hermit and avoids contact with people. If I can talk him into seeing you, just go slow and I think you'll do okay. Even if he won't take you on as an apprentice, talking with him will be interesting, to say the least."

Matilda was excited, "I'd like to talk to him. Where is his office? I want to meet him. Tell me how to find him."

Doc explained, "Hiram doesn't have an office. He stays in his log cabin. It's about ten miles west of here, up on

Picked Mountain. He rarely leaves the place and doesn't have any visitors, as far as I know, but I may be able to talk him into seeing you. He has a phone but doesn't always answer when it rings. The dirt road up to his place is pretty rough and narrow."

Doc asked Zelda to pull his chart and get the phone number. Then he continued, "I'll call and explain your predicament, Matilda. Perhaps he'll be willing to consider taking you on as an apprentice."

Matilda relaxed a little as she considered the possibility of reaching her goal in just a year, and without leaving Lakewood. Zelda handed Doc the chart. He nodded his thanks, looked at the chart, smiled at Matilda, and dialed the number. It rang several times before Hiram answered, "It's your nickel, shoot."

Doc chuckled, "I wish it was still a nickel, Hiram. This is Doc Williams. How're you doing?"

The loud answer made Doc move the receiver away from his ear, "Getting by, but got more backaches than an old stone wall. Getting old and crotchety. What's up Doc?"

Doc held one finger to his lips, and pressed the speaker on his phone so the two women could hear, and said," You may remember Matilda, my medical assistant. She took your x-ray when you came in a few months ago."

Hiram's voice boomed from the speaker, "You mean that long cool drink of water?"

Doc glanced at Matilda and smiled, "I guess you remember her, although I wouldn't describe her that way. She's very attractive, tall and thin, with light brown hair."

"A slab-sided cracker-ass is what I remember. What about her?"

9

Doc grimaced at that remark and continued, "Well, she's decided to become a detective. She's one of the brightest people I know. I told her there's no one better to show her the ropes than you. Would you be willing to talk with her?"

Hiram boomed again, "Talk's cheap and I've got time. A couple unsolved cases are bugging me. My right hand's been itching all day, so I knew I was going to meet someone. I'll be glad to yarn with her. We grow too soon old and too late smart. My advice costs nothing and that's probably what it's worth."

"Thanks, Hiram. Is there a good time for her to come see you?"

"I'm here most of the time. The road's still passable, if she starts in the right rut. Tell her to come alone, and just yell if I don't answer the door. If she's not alone, she won't see me."

"I'll let her know. I expect she'll be there tomorrow. Thanks, Hiram."

Doc hung up the phone and looked at Matilda and Zelda, who were grinning from ear to ear. The three friends broke into simultaneous laughter. When it subsided, Doc said, "I think you heard. Usually I don't put people on the speaker without telling them, but I wanted you to know what you're getting into. He's expecting you tomorrow. You'll enjoy talking with him, even if you don't strike a deal. Do you know the Picked Mountain Road out of Bill's Mills?"

Matilda still chuckled as she said, "Yes. I've seen the sign."

"Hiram's house is the last one on the road. If it rains tonight, don't try it. The narrow dirt road up the mountain is steep and muddy when it's wet. There are no guardrails and the road is cut into the side of the mountain with a sheer drop-off in some places. I don't think he was kidding about getting started in the right rut."

"Thanks, Doc. Zelda knew you could help, and I didn't know which way to turn. At least there's a chance I can become a detective while staying near my friends and living in the comfort of my home."

Doc smiled, "Let us know how it goes. We both want to know how the "cracker-ass" makes out. I enjoy talking with Hiram, and I think you will. I'm going to leave you two now. It's time to go home to my family. I promised the boys I'd play catch with them before supper. Good luck and good night."

CHAPTER TWO

Hiram's Problem

It was raining the next morning, but Matilda had just installed new snow treads for the winter and felt her maroon Buick Roadmaster could go anywhere. She found the Picked Mountain sign and started up the narrow dirt road. The heavy car's wheels spun on some steep places, but kept climbing up the rough road until it ended beside a large log cabin. She parked beside a muddy Jeep, got out and looked around. The house was moss-covered and looked as if it had germinated from the soil itself, standing on a small flat area with a rocky cliff behind it and a steep drop off beyond the old Jeep. A face flashed briefly in one window, then disappeared.

Matilda looked around. The mist cleared enough to show the White Mountains over the tops of the trees below. She stood beside her car, admiring the view, when the cabin door opened. A thin man with a scraggy white beard stepped out and said in a loud voice, "You're not as bright as Doc suggested, driving up here in a drizzle. Fools go where angels fear to tread. I heard your tires spinning a half-mile away. You could have waited until afternoon. Rain starting before seven will stop before eleven. Morning showers and old women's dancing don't last long."

Matilda smiled and said, "Hello, Hiram. Can I come in out of the rain?"

Hiram held the door open for her, "You're here now. Come on in. I'm making some tea. Have a seat and I'll be with you in two shakes of a dead lamb's tail."

"That sounds good. Thanks for seeing me."

The cabin was comfortably furnished, neat and clean. Matilda sat at the table made of thick planks and observed Hiram as he got out a teapot and started tea brewing. She noticed a limp that her nurses training interpreted as a stiffened left knee joint. His wiry body moved briskly and deftly as he got out cups and saucers. Matilda estimated his age at about sixty years. His face had strong chiseled features, only partly hidden by the beard.

She looked around the cabin and saw a large oak roll-top desk, with every cubbyhole stuffed with papers. Two long board shelves over it bowed with the weight of an assortment of books. On all four sides of the big room, she noticed deep notches cut into the logs. They were wide on the inside and cut all the way through, leaving a vertical slit on the outside. They reminded her of the slit windows in the old fort at Pemaquid Point. Doc said Hiram made his cabin into a fortress. That must be what he meant. A pistol in a shoulder holster hung on a peg beside the door and a rifle rested on pegs over the door. A gun rack beside the desk held an assortment of rifles and shotguns. The floor was clean, and the dishes neatly stacked on shelves. Matilda decided Hiram was a good housekeeper. He looked tough as nails, and physically fit in spite of the serious injuries Doc treated.

Hiram put the teacups, cream and sugar on the table, poured two cups of tea, then walked around the room, stopping to look out one window after another. He slowly opened the door a crack and listened, then returned and sat down before saying anything more. He watched her put a teaspoon of sugar in her tea, and said, "Doc said you want to be a detective. Why?"

"My father was a lawyer and a judge. We discussed many legal issues before he died. I've always been interested in the law, but didn't have the background to go to law school. My training was in nursing and x-ray. I like solving problems, and helped two doctors by discussing difficult diagnostic problems with them. They knew the answers, but I helped them by focusing on the process and the personalities involved. I'm fifty years old, and it's time for me to get started in detective work, if I'm ever going to do it. I set up my office and made plans before I realized what I had to do to get a license. I don't need to be paid, but would like to work with you as an apprentice so I can get my own private investigator license in a year."

Hiram listened without any expression, and sat looking at her for a long time before he said, "The smart man knows how little he really knows. It'll be a challenge for me. More men rust out than wear out. Before we make any decisions, let's talk about a case that's been bothering me for the past month. Would you like to hear about it?"

"Very much. Please tell me about it."

"OK, two heads are better than one, even if one's a sheep's head. You remember hearing about a Dr. Price who was shot in his hunting camp in Greenville last September on opening day of bird hunting season?"

"I remember reading about that. The Lakewood News said he was alone in his cabin on Moosehead Lake. The rest of his hunting party came the next day and found him. The Sheriff and Medical Examiner ruled it an accidental death. The papers said his shotgun apparently discharged accidentally, killing him instantly. Is there something suspicious about his death? Do you think it might have been a suicide?"

"No! Murder!"

"Are you sure?"

Hiram almost shouted, "Is the Pope catholic? Do bears shit in the woods? Of course I'm sure."

Matilda smiled as she said, "I didn't mean to upset you. Tell me about it. You must have information not reported in the papers, at least not in what I remember."

Hiram grumbled loudly, "When's the last time the papers got anything right? They report anything they hear, if it sells papers. I never read newspapers anymore. They're as useless as a cork anchor."

"I agree. Whenever I know the facts about a situation, the Lakewood News always reports a distorted picture. How are you involved in this case?"

"Dr. Price's brother is a lawyer who lives in New Jersey, and knew me when I worked there. One of his clients, an ex-marine, was charged with a crime he didn't commit. He was passing by when a man near him was shot. He ducked into a doorway until the car drove away, then ran over, picked up the gun, and stood protecting the injured man until the police arrived. They arrested him because he was there. He swore at the officers, and tried to tell them what he saw, but they weren't listening. When they forced him face down on the street and put handcuffs on him, he got upset and called the police 'pigs', and worse. He was innocent, but they had to arrest someone."

As Hiram told the story, Matilda studied him. His regular features and bright blue eyes made his thin face attractive. The scraggy gray beard covered a strong chin. His muscles rippled under his shirt as he talked animatedly. She tried to imagine the man he was before the injuries. He was still a rugged handsome man. Matilda had resisted all

15

offers of marriage since her husband died, but she enjoyed good company, spending vacation weeks with several different interesting men. Even though Hiram was ten years older than she was, she hoped they could become colleagues. Working with him for a year would give her the credentials needed to get her own private investigator license. Doc was right. Hiram was a fascinating character.

She listened carefully as Hiram continued his story, "The next morning the guy was sober as a judge, and stuck to his story. I worked on the case and identified the real criminal. The guy's lawyer, Dr. Price's brother, was very grateful. After that, he called me whenever he had questions about police procedures. He helped me get out of the hospital and transported to Maine. He's one of the very few people who know that I'm still alive.

"He came to Maine for the funeral, and didn't believe the story he got from the sheriff. When the police didn't investigate, or even suspect foul play, he came to see me. He's solid as a brick and sharp as they come. He knew his brother would never be careless with a gun, and certainly wouldn't commit suicide. He agreed to pay my hourly rate, and offered me a big bonus if I would find the killer and bring him to justice. I know who did it, but damned if I can prove it."

Trying not to sound too eager, Matilda said, "I'd like to help you if I can. Please tell me more about it."

Hiram sat very still, then jumped up and went to the front window. After scanning the outside for a minute, he opened the door a crack and stood listening. Matilda heard the faint sound of the motor that probably startled him. She watched as he stepped outside, then returned, closed the door and came back to his chair. He looked at her and said,

"Airplane, sight seeing." as if that explained everything, then continued, "Okay, Dr. Price was a meticulous surgeon who fussed about every detail, even to being compulsive about some things. If a man brought a loaded shotgun into his camp, he made him go outside and unload it. It's beyond me how anyone could think that a man like that would put a loaded shotgun against his chest to clean it, and accidentally hit the trigger. The local deputy sheriff is a dim bulb. He just looked around and called it an accident. A man was shot in the chest, and he didn't even secure the crime scene. He let the other men bring in their dogs and spend the night there, ruining any evidence there might have been. Damn a fool, a drunk man will get sober. That deputy is as useless as a cut cat. His boss, Sheriff Darcy, either is hiding something, or is so crooked that when he dies, they'll have to screw him into the ground. He wouldn't give me the time of day. He looked awful, his eyes like two cane holes in a cow flap, as if he hadn't slept for a week. He assured me it was an accidental death, but I knew he lied through his teeth. He's hiding something. There's no way this was an accident."

Matilda mused, "Is suicide a possibility?"

"No way! Dr. Price loved life. He hit on every pretty nurse, and even propositioned some of his women patients. He appeared to care for his wife and children. He had no financial problems. His brother said they planned a scuba diving trip together to the Great Barrier Reef next month, and discussed it on the phone every week. The doctor was never depressed and certainly not suicidal. I talked with his partner, his office manager and his wife. They all agreed, he loved life and enjoyed every minute of it. Suicide is even less likely than an accident. If it was not an accident, and it couldn't have been, and not suicide, which is equally impossible, it had to be murder. It stands out like the nose on your face."

"You said you know who did it. Who is that?"

"Let's not get the cart before the horse. First, let me tell you what I discovered and the way I found it."

Matilda smiled, sipped her tea and relaxed. Doc was right. Hiram certainly was an interesting a character. She looked forward to working with him. Hiram sat deep in thought for a minute, and continued, "Dr. Price's wife knew about his attraction to younger women, but also knew he loved her and the children. Even after they were engaged, he continued to date other girls. When she confronted him with this, he said he loved her, but still enjoyed the chase and conquest game he'd played for years. If she would have him as he was, he'd be the best possible husband, with that one exception. She agreed, as long as he was discrete and didn't cause a scandal."

"That's an interesting arrangement. I know some women who are aware of their husband's peccadilloes and say nothing, and others who should recognize it and don't."

"There's none so blind as they who will not see. The doctor's wife accepted it because he was otherwise such a good husband. She loved him dearly, and was devastated by his death. She had her doubts about it being an accident, but knew it wasn't suicide, so accepted Sheriff Darcy's report that he was alone at the time of his death. Her husband left her well off, but he was just at the peak of his career and making a big income. There was no reason for her to want him dead. I'm certain she wasn't involved in his murder."

"But you do have a suspect?"

"Suspect is a weasel word the lawyers use. I don't suspect, I know the murderer, but I can't prove it yet. I'll get the goods on him somehow."

Hiram sipped his tea and stared into the distance, then got up and walked around the cabin, glancing out each of the windows. Matilda watched him, and waited for him to continue, not wanting to disturb his train of thought. Finally, he looked back at her and said, "The doctor was in a partnership with another surgeon. They had a good practice and covered for each other. The partner, Dr. Galliano, seemed very upset at the death of his partner. He cancelled all the scheduled surgery, and told the office staff they could go on half time for a month while he was in mourning. I thought the arrangement was unusual, and went to see Dr. Galliano. When he heard I was a private investigator, he refused to see me. I knew he was hiding something. I talked to Florence Gifford, the office manager, and found he didn't plan to reopen the office, but gave all the staff notice so they could find other jobs. She told me Dr. Galliano did very little surgery for the two months before his partner's death, and the staff suspected he was planning to retire. She told me an insurance adjuster had come and asked questions. After some persuasion, she gave me the name of the insurance company. I've done some work for the Bell Underwriters before, and even have an open case under contract. We can discuss that later."

"So you work for an insurance company now?"

"Not exclusively, only on a case by case basis. Anyway, I contacted them and told them I had some information they might need. They were eager to see me. They told me the two partners had mutual insurance coverage, paying $500,000 to the other in case of death or permanent disability. The policy had an accidental death provision, paying double the face amount. Dr. Galliano was going to get a million dollars. Bell Underwriters offered to pay me my hourly rate to determine whether or not the death was accidental. Their policy has an exclusion clause for suicide, and will pay nothing if that can be proven. From their investigation, it looked more like suicide than an accident, but they had to rely on the report of the sheriff and the medical examiner, both of whom called it an accidental death. When I called Dr. Galliano again, I told him I was working for the insurance company who would withhold any payment until I completed my investigation. He then agreed to see me."

"Dr. Galliano met me at his home, a large estate on the ocean in Cape Elizabeth. A butler, who looked more like a wrestler, escorted me to a library. Dr. Galliano remained seated in his reclining chair throughout the interview. He answered all my questions without hesitation, cool as a cucumber. His facial expression didn't change at all when I tried to startle him by telling him I was employed to investigate the possibility of suicide or murder. I was impressed with the way he controlled his emotions. He kept rolling something between his thumb and index finger while we talked. Otherwise, he seemed perfectly calm and relaxed. I left without anything except a deepening suspicion that he was involved. Still waters run deep. He was holding his cards pretty close to his vest. He acted guilty as sin."

"What made you suspicious of him? He was part of a successful practice, and doing very well financially. Why would he want to harm his partner?"

"His living high on the hog led me to check his financial standing. Through the insurance company, I was able to get a complete financial statement. Unlike his partner, Dr. Galliano spent it as fast as he got it. Money was in one hand and out the other. He was a two-time loser, making big alimony payments to two prior wives. He lived like a king. His bank balance was minimal, and his credit cards were near their generous limits. He needed money, and the death of his partner gave him a million dollars. That's motive enough for anyone."

"But opportunity? Didn't he have to cover the practice while his partner went on a hunting trip? He couldn't have been in Portland and Greenville at the same time."

"You're right, but I checked his schedule. He didn't have any surgery scheduled while his partner was away. He was on call, but on a beeper. He could answer calls from anywhere. I talked with Florence Gifford, their office manager, again. Dr. Galliano hadn't operated for a month. He did only office work, while his partner did all the surgery. She thought Dr. Galliano might have been ill, but no one said anything about it to her. Florence said she called his house and talked with him whenever she had questions. He stopped by the office most mornings, but otherwise took calls at home. She didn't keep a log of telephone calls, and couldn't remember if she'd talked with Dr. Galliano on the day Dr. Price died. It's a three-hour drive from Portland to Greenville. He could have gone and come back without anyone knowing."

"So he had motive and opportunity. You need a lot more than that to charge him with murder. Did you talk with the sheriff about your suspicions?"

"I sure did, and almost got kicked out on my ear. Sheriff Darcy didn't want to hear anything about my ideas. He said the case was closed, and I was interfering with police business. He was as restless as a cat on a hot tin roof all the time I was there. He's hiding something, or someone paid him to ignore the evidence. In New Jersey, I'd suspect the mob got to him, but that's not likely here. I can recognize a crooked cop and know when someone is covering up something. Darcy knows a lot more than he's willing to talk about."

"If he was paid off, why? And by whom?"

"It had to be Dr. Galliano. I know he's the murderer, but I can't prove it. He had motive, opportunity and no alibi for the time of the murder. He was too cool, calm and collected when I talked with him. I know he's hiding something. If you can tell me where to go from here, I'll be pleased to take you on as my apprentice."

Matilda thought for a minute, and said, "One thing occurred to me. You said Dr. Galliano sat in a chair and had no change in his facial expression all the time you talked with him, but you did notice him rolling something between his thumb and index finger."

Hiram growled, "Yeah, he's stone faced. He keeps his emotions as tight as the bark on a tree. It was like talking to a statue. Back in New Jersey, I'd have him in the cooler and sweat him until he talked. That door's shut to me now. That sphinx is in total control and not going to let anything out."

Matilda leaned forward. "There's another possibility. He stopped operating a month before his partner died, and closed the office when he got the news. There may be a reason for both. The expressionless face and pill-rolling tremor are symptoms of advanced Parkinson's disease. I think his hands probably shake too much to function as a surgeon. Someone in the operating room must have noticed. I think he's disabled."

"Tell me about Parkinson's disease. Is it curable?"

"No, it's progressive. As a doctor, he would have taken medication to control it as long as it could be kept in check. Apparently, Dr. Galliano's condition was too far along to continue working. That's why he sat in his chair and didn't try to walk while you were there. He would have shuffled and had trouble walking. If he couldn't control the pill-rolling tremor of his hand, I doubt that he could have attacked and killed a vigorous man like his partner. It's unlikely he was the killer, if it was murder."

"It was murder! I'm sure, and he did it. From what you tell me, there's even more reason for Dr. Galliano to be the murderer. With his disability increasing and likely to be permanent, the insurance policy would have paid his partner, leaving him with nothing. Your information about his illness increases his motive ten fold. Somehow, he had to arrange the killing to look like an accident. If he couldn't do it, he must have hired someone. Perhaps he sent that muscular butler of his. He could have done it."

"We don't seem any nearer to having the evidence we need to charge anyone. You told the sheriff your suspicions and he threw you out of his office. Where do we go from here?"

"You said, 'we'. I like that. You've helped me already. I didn't know about Parkinson's disease. Let's work on this together. For the next year you're my apprentice, if you still want to work with an old reprobate."

Matilda smiled, "Just let me know what you want me to do first."

Hiram jumped up and walked around looking out the windows again. He peered through one of the silts for a minute, then walked back, sat down and resumed as if there was no interruption, "I've worked alone for so long, I need to think. It's different, pulling in a double harness again. You might talk with Florence Gifford again, and see if you can get more information. She must know who treated him for his Parkinson's disease. An office manager would know if the doctors talked about Dr. Galliano admitting his disability and letting Dr. Price collect on the insurance."

"I'll do that. Anything else?"

"I'm not sure I got all the information available from the widow. She was very upset when I talked with her. I'd like you to meet with her. See if you can get more information than I did. It's worth a try."

"OK. Anything else?"

"Sheriff Darcy clammed up when I asked him questions. He's hiding something. I wondered if he talked with Dr. Galliano. The deputy might tell you. Maybe you could see him and butter him up. That's a lot of running around."

"No problem for a full time apprentice detective. I'll get started, and write everything down. Can we get together and talk whenever I have questions?"

"Come anytime, but phone me first. I don't like surprises. I'm glad Doc suggested you come see me. We'll make a great team."

Matilda drove down the mountain road, thinking, "Now I'm an apprentice detective, investigating a murder. Wow!"

She hurried along, her mind sorting out the case she was sharing with Hiram. Suddenly her car slid sideways. She jammed on the brakes and stopped on the edge of a deep ditch. She sat for a minute getting her courage back, then put the car in reverse and backed up until it was again on the dirt road. When she stopped shaking, she thought, "Hiram was right about picking the right rut."

As she started down the mountain again, she drove slowly and watched the road carefully until she reached the paved road. Things were going too well to take any chances.

Hiram watched her leave, carefully scanned the area and listened until the sound of her engine faded away. Satisfied that he was alone, he returned to the cabin and sat in his rocking chair. He was impressed. Matilda seemed as bright as Doc said, smart as a whip. She was too thin for his taste, but was well filled out in the right places. He always felt a police officer shouldn't have a permanent involvement with a woman. It was too easy to get killed, as he almost found out. But now, there was no reason to be inhibited. If he weren't a cripple, he would welcome a personal relationship. At least, he had someone vigorous to do some legwork for him. This was going to work out well. She could do the traveling and he could stay out of sight. He'd lived like a hermit for two years while gaining his strength back. Except for the lawyer and the police commissioner, no one in New Jersey knew he was alive, or gave a damn. That gave him some security, but maybe it was time to get back into the world and meet some people. Living alone and isolated met his needs for the past two years. Pretending to be a cantankerous hermit kept the local folk from getting too curious. There was a lot to consider about the future. Matilda had awakened long suppressed thoughts and desires.

The Calzoni robbery could wait. All his instincts warned him of danger there. Matilda would limit his exposure if she did all the questioning from now on. He already felt apprehensive, although there was no evidence that Richard Calzoni had any connection to the New Jersey gangster with that name. Hiram hoped his hermit guise and rustic expressions might fool anyone looking for him, but he still used his right name. Probably that was a mistake. He sat rocking in his chair deep in thought for the two hours, only occasionally jumping up to look out the windows.

CHAPTER THREE

Matilda Asks Florence

Matilda sat in her big leather swivel chair and thought about the case, making notes in a spiral bound notebook. Hiram suggested three interviews. Florence Gifford, the doctor's office manager, would be easiest to interview. Dr. Price's widow should not be difficult, but she might not know anything. On the other hand, the police always consider the spouse a prime suspect in any murder. Women often know more than men think they do.

Sheriff Darcy seemed to be hiding something. That was the challenge. Matilda decided to get as much information as she could before seeing the sheriff. Knowing the right questions to ask was important.

Matilda called Dr. Galliano's office and listened to a pleasant voice on a recording, "*You have reached the office of Doctors Galliano and Price. The office is closed. If this concerns an outstanding bill, please call Florence Gifford at 666-2468. If you need medical care, please call the Maine Medical Center Healthfinders for referral. If you need medical records forwarded, at the sound of the beep, please carefully state your name, the date of your last visit, and the name of the physician to receive the records. You will receive a release form in the mail. When this is signed and returned, the records will be forwarded. Have a good day.*"

Matilda called the billing number and Florence Gifford answered on the first ring, "Dr. Galliano's office, this is Miss Gifford. How may I help you?"

"Hello Miss Gifford. This is Matilda Parker. I work with Hiram Murphy. He saw you when investigating the death of Dr. Price for the insurance company. There are a few more details to confirm. May I see you sometime soon?"

Florence hesitated briefly, and said, "I told him everything I know, but I'll be glad to see you. The office is closed but come to the back door and ring the bell. I'll let you in. I'm here weekdays from eight to twelve. What time is best for you?"

"I can come a little after eight tomorrow morning, if that's all right."

"That's fine. I'll see you then. Goodbye."

Matilda found the address in the telephone book. The office was a one-story brick building across the road from the hospital. She parked in the empty parking lot a little after eight. A pleasant middle-aged woman opened the door at Matilda's ring. She welcomed Matilda and offered her coffee, which she accepted. Matilda observed Florence as she moved around the room. She seemed relaxed, but had a slight strain in her voice as she asked, "What can I tell you? How can I help the insurance company?"

Matilda opened her spiral notepad, glanced at it, and said, "They want as much detail as possible on the arrangement between the doctors, and how they worked. The company wants to know if the doctors shared the work load equally."

"Yes they did, ever since they started practice together twenty years ago. I started as their office nurse and became their office manager. They did make some changes recently. Dr. Galliano did less surgery and more office work, while Dr. Price was busier in the OR. It was by mutual agreement.

They asked us to schedule things that way. Dr. Galliano did no surgery during the month before Dr. Price died."

"Do you know why the change in activity occurred? Was Dr. Galliano ill?"

Florence hesitated briefly before saying, "I suspected that he might have the flu or something, but nothing was ever said. Dr. Galliano slowed down in his walk and talk, as if he were conserving his energy. I think he's going to retire."

Matilda watched Florence carefully as she asked. "The prior investigator who saw Dr. Galliano thought he might have Parkinson's disease. Is that a possibility?"

Florence hesitated again, as if considering the possibility, and said, "Now that you mention it, that is a possibility. I didn't think much about it at the time, but I noticed an occasional intention tremor a couple months ago. That could be the reason he stopped operating. I should have recognized it, but it came on so slowly that I didn't think about Parkinson's. Is that important?"

"Yes, the policy pays the remaining partner on the death or disability of the other partner. If Dr. Galliano became permanently disabled, the policy would have paid Dr. Price. The company is concerned that Dr. Price died accidentally just before a claim could have been made in his favor. The accidental death doubles the award paid to Dr. Galliano. So, as you can see, the company needs all the facts before paying the claim."

Florence seemed tense and a little evasive as she said, "I knew nothing about their insurance or business arrangement. They had an equal partnership as far as I know."

Matilda raised her eyebrows, and spent a moment looking at her notebook. The office manager would certainly know the details of the partnership. Finally, she looked up and asked, "Was Dr Galliano seeing an internist or neurologist?"

"Yes. He had regular checkups with an internist, and was seeing him more frequently this past year. I'll give you his name. I don't know if he'll tell you anything."

"Thanks. Dr. Galliano was the major beneficiary of Dr. Price's death. We need all the details we can get to eliminate any possibility of foul play."

Florence stood up suddenly and stared at Matilda. "What do you mean *foul play?* Dr. Price had an awful accident. I'm sure Dr. Galliano wasn't involved in his death. They were the best of friends, in addition to being partners. That's not even plausible."

Matilda made a note and studied her notebook for a while to let Florence calm down, and asked, "Were there any threats on Dr. Price's life? Did he have any enemies? Can you think of anyone who would want to hurt him?"

Florence sat down and relaxed a little. Finally, she said, "Not really. Sometimes there were young women who seemed upset about something, but no one ever threatened him, as far as I know. There was one belligerent older woman who yelled at him a month ago. I didn't hear what they were saying, but she stormed out of here and almost took the door off the hinges. She was twice my size and I just got out of the way. After she left, I asked Dr. Price if he needed a chart to make notes. He just gave a grim smile and said, "It's not about a patient.""

"Do you have her name? Did she have an appointment?"

"No, she just stormed in and walked into his office without knocking. Fortunately, he was alone. She wore a dark blue dress and looked like a police officer. She was very upset. I never saw her before, nor have I seen her since. I don't really want to, either. She scared me."

"Do you remember when that was?"

"It was a Friday morning, the week before the doctor's hunting vacation."

Matilda made a note in her notepad, and asked, "Is there anyone else who was upset or angry with him"

"No. All his patients loved him. He was kind and considerate to the employees. I can't imagine anyone wanting to harm him. It was a horrible accident. They do happen, you know."

"Yes, I do know. Is there anything else you can tell me to help the insurance company?"

"Not that I can think of. Leave your card and I'll call if I think of anything."

"Please call the senior investigator, Mr. Hiram Murphy, if you think of anything. Do you still have his card?"

"Yes, it's on file."

"Thanks a lot. I'll call you if the insurance company has any more questions."

Matilda had several things to consider on her drive home. She stopped at a rest area, consulted her notebook, and made a list of things to discuss with Hiram. She decided to get a small tape recorder to help her remember, and even record interviews, if the opportunity arose.

First, she needed some business cards. This would require consultation with Hiram to be sure the wording was correct. The thought of advancing her new career with business cards gave her a feeling of accomplishment. Doc or her friends could offer one of her cards to anyone needing an investigation.

Second, there was one large, aggressive, middle-aged woman who was very upset at Dr. Price about something. Her identity was obscure, and she might have no bearing on the case, but it would be helpful to know why she was upset. A woman as angry as Florence described, had to have a reason. Hiram would know how to evaluate that.

Third, Florence agreed with the possibility that Dr. Galliano has Parkinson's disease. It was odd that she hadn't recognized it earlier. Florence knew a lot more than she admitted. Matilda was an office manager too long to believe that Florence didn't know everything about the doctor's arrangements. Dr. Galliano's illness was so far advanced that Hiram could describe the classic signs of Parkinson's disease from one interview. Florence certainly knew his diagnosis and prognosis. Why would she deny it? Maybe Hiram would have an explanation for that.

Fourth, she had the name of the internist who was treating Dr. Galliano. If they needed confirmation of his diagnosis, Doc could get a report from the internist, or Dr. Galliano might sign a record release form, if he had nothing to hide. The diagnosis seemed perfectly clear, so there seemed little reason to pursue confirmation.

Fifth, Florence was adamant that Dr. Galliano was innocent of any involvement. She might be covering for him, or perhaps Hiram was barking up the wrong tree. Her reaction to the suggestion of foul play was excessive. She tried to hide her feelings but they boiled over. There might be some collusion between those two.

Matilda drove back to Lakewood, turning these questions over in her mind. She decided it was good that she had a mentor to sort things out. Maybe the doctor's widow or the sheriff would fill in the blanks. For the first time in years, she felt challenged mentally. Competing in national bridge tournaments was becoming routine. There was so much to learn in becoming a detective. There were real life-and-death matters to sort out. Doc must feel this way at times.

CHAPTER FOUR

Matilda Asks Mrs. Price

Mrs. Price was very gracious when Matilda called to say she was collecting information for an insurance company. They agreed upon meeting at ten o'clock the next morning. The house was in the best part of Falmouth Foreside, large but not pretentious. A wide driveway and a three-car garage flanked the two story colonial house. The beautifully landscaped grounds and neatly mowed lawns matched the rest of the upscale neighborhood. Matilda was on time and welcomed into the warm living room by a petite woman with a pleasant smile. She led Matilda to a large easy chair by the fireplace, and sat in a smaller wing backed chair facing her.

Mrs. Price sat very erect with her ankles crossed, and said pleasantly, "Thank you for coming, Mrs. Parker. What insurance company do you represent?"

"I represent the Bell Underwriters who have the business insurance policy for the Galliano and Price partnership. I would like to offer my condolences for your loss. I regret having to bother you at this time. Do you mind answering some questions?"

"No, I don't mind. I'm still numb, but if I can help, I will."

"Thank you. Did you know the partnership had a policy to pay the surviving partner?"

"No, I'm sorry. I knew very little about my husband's business arrangements. We didn't discuss that."

Matilda tilted her head and asked, "You knew nothing about the partnership?"

"Very little. Oh, one time Franklin told me that Saul, Dr. Galliano, would be responsible for all the debts and assets of the practice if anything happened to him. He wanted me to know there would be no income or expense from the practice if he should die. Saul would take care of everything. I'm not much of a businesswoman. Franklin managed all our financial affairs. We spent our time talking about the children and enjoying each other. Is there some problem with their financial arrangement?"

Matilda said reassuringly, "The partnership agreements are not our concern. The insurance policy has a provision to pay double indemnity if the death of a partner is the result of an accident. The company has to be certain there is no possibility that the death was other than accidental. Please understand, this is routine but necessary. Do you mind if I confirm some of the facts we were given?"

"I'll help in any way I can. There's not much I can tell you. I wasn't there. My information all came from his friends who found him. The sheriff said it was accidental, without any question. What can I tell you?"

"Just background information. It's all assessed in the home office. For instance, did your husband have any enemies? Was he ever threatened as far as you know?"

Mrs. Price narrowed her eyes and stiffened, as she said, "No. There were never any threats of which I was aware. Everyone loved my husband. Sometimes too many young women loved him, but that was never a real problem. He had no enemies."

"Were there any telephone calls, or anyone visiting, that upset him?"

"No, not that I can recall. Oh, I did hear him raise his voice on the telephone once. He acted upset. When I raised my eyebrows, he covered the mouthpiece and said, 'The lady is deaf and I have to shout'. Then, he answered her questions, usually with one word. I remember him saying loudly, "I am sorry to hear that" and "Come to the office tomorrow and we'll talk about it."

Matilda opened her notebook and made a note before she asked, "Do you remember when that was, exactly?"

"It was a Thursday evening, our bridge night, the week before he left for his hunting trip. It was almost seven o'clock. I remember, because I thought we might be late if he talked too long. Is that important?"

"I'm not sure what the company may think is important. I just collect the data and report to them. One other thing, how did the partners get along?"

Mrs. Price's face brightened as she said, "Oh, they were great friends. We saw a lot of each other until Saul's divorce about two years ago. I haven't seen him much since then. I still see his former wife sometimes. She says he pays her alimony on time. I know Franklin and Saul admired and respected each other. They were best friends since medical school."

Matilda made a couple notes on her notepad, and asked, "Are you aware that Dr. Galliano was not doing surgery and working only in the office?"

"No. As I said, I haven't seen Saul for several months. Franklin didn't mention anything about an illness. I hope he's all right. Franklin's death must have been an awful shock to him. He and Franklin were very close."

Matilda said, "Thank you very much. That's all the questions they wanted me to ask. Unless you can think of anything else to help us, I'll go and make my report."

"I can't think of anything. I hope I've been helpful. I miss him terribly. He was a good husband and father. It's hard to think of him gone."

Matilda stood and said, "I'm sorry for your loss. It must be very difficult for your family at this time. Thank you very much for your help."

Matilda walked to her car, thinking about the gracious lady. Mrs. Price seemed very open and honest. Matilda remembered the many months it took her to get over the loss of her husband. Mrs. Price was bearing up well under the tragic circumstances. Nothing in her manner raised any suspicions about her involvement in a crime, if indeed a crime was committed.

CHAPTER FIVE

Matilda Asks Sheriff Darcy

Matilda had plenty of time to collect her thoughts on the long drive to Greenville. When she called the sheriff's office that morning, the deputy told her Sheriff Darcy was usually in the office afternoons from two until six. She didn't ask for an appointment, but said she'd stop in that afternoon to give him some information. The deputy didn't ask questions and she didn't offer anything more.

There were still more questions than answers. Dr. Galliano looked less like a suspect, although he could have hired someone to kill Dr. Price, and paid off the sheriff. It was a lot to assume, in view of Dr. Galliano's limited mobility. This theory required a conspiracy including the doctor, the murderer, the sheriff and maybe the medical examiner. This seemed too complicated to be reasonable. Dr. Galliano did benefit from Dr. Price's death, but that was the only reason to suspect him. There had to be another explanation.

The large woman in a dark blue dress, who berated Dr. Price in his office the Friday before he went on vacation, was probably the same person his wife heard him shouting at the night before. If she could be identified, that might lead to more clues and maybe some answers. There was something familiar about the description of the woman, although the connection didn't come to her. Even though suicide or an accident was unlikely, she could see no evidence pointing to a murder. Perhaps Hiram was wrong in his assessment. He said Sheriff Darcy seemed to be hiding something. Today might bring some answers.

At two o'clock Matilda arrived at the Sheriff's office and met the deputy. He was pleasant, and asked her to have a seat. He expected Sheriff Darcy any minute. Matilda sat in a straight chair in the sparsely furnished office. Beside a big corkboard filled with wanted notices, she saw a picture with a black cloth draped around it. Matilda walked over and studied the photograph of a pretty, young woman in a nurse's uniform and cap. She asked the deputy, "It seems you're in mourning. Is the pretty girl related to you?"

"That's Sheriff Darcy's daughter's picture. She died last month."

"Oh, I'm sorry to hear that. What happened?"

The deputy looked around, and answered in a conspirital whisper, "She killed herself. The Sheriff is still quite upset about it. He visits her grave every day. That may be where he is now."

"That's awful. I'm very sorry. Was she ill or depressed?"

"I think it was a love affair gone sour. She was fine until just a few days before, when she came in and told her father he had to help her. They talked, but I don't know what they said. Two days later, she hanged herself. It was in all the papers."

Matilda wondered about the deputy offering all this information, but then, she remembered Hiram calling him a dim bulb and other less complimentary things. She decided to keep him talking, asking, "Did her father try to help her? What do you suppose she wanted him to do?"

"He called the State Health Nurse and talked with her, but that was the day before his daughter died. The State

Health Nurse talked with him several times after that. She hasn't been in for the past couple of weeks. He's been very quiet ever since his daughter died. Maybe you shouldn't mention it. It makes him upset."

"I understand. One more question, Did the Sheriff talk with Dr Galliano?"

"He talked with someone with an Italian name, but I don't think you have it right. I wrote it down on my calendar. Just a minute, here it is. No the name was Calzoni, not what you said. Here he comes now."

The sheriff dropped some papers on his deputy's desk, glanced at Matilda, and walked into his office without speaking. The deputy said, "I'll tell him you want to see him. Can I tell him what it's about?"

"I have some information on the death of Dr. Price. I need him to confirm the data so my insurance company can pay the claim."

The deputy nodded, went into the sheriff's office and came back out saying, "He said he can give you a couple minutes. Go right in."

Matilda went into the sheriff's office and stood before his desk. When he didn't look up, she sat in the nearest chair and waited. The sheriff was a muscular man of medium height. His face looked drawn and pale, as if he had some chronic illness. Matilda was trying to think of a diagnosis, when he pushed his papers aside and looked up with red-rimmed eyes, and said, "What information do you have?"

Matilda decided to ignore the deputy's advice and said, "First, I'd like to offer my condolences for your bereavement. It was a tragedy."

The sheriff didn't relax, but said, "Thanks. I don't have much time. Get to the point. I gave a full report to the insurance company. What can you tell me that I don't already know?"

Matilda took a deep breath and decided direct confrontation was the only way to shake him up. She made a connection in her head. Gloria Ingraham was the Maine State Health Nurse in this area. She was a very large woman who fit the description Florence gave her. It was worth a try. With some trepidation, but speaking with firm conviction, she said, "I talked to his wife and his office manager. A large woman, who they feel was a State Health Nurse, threatened him the week before he died. You didn't mention Gloria Ingraham in your report. You saw her before and after Dr. Price died. Please tell me about it."

The sheriff stiffened and then slowly leaned back in his chair, staring at Matilda. He remained silent for more than a minute before saying, "Gloria had nothing to do with Dr. Price's accident. She was here to console me about my daughter, and that's none of your business. I don't need to tell you anything. You may leave now."

Her suspicions were confirmed. The State Health Nurse was Gloria. Matilda decided to play her hunch a little further, "Threats on Dr. Price's life are not important? Gloria went to his office and accused Dr. Price of causing your daughter's death. Isn't that important? Unless you modify your report to include the facts you know, the Attorney General will be pleased to investigate and determine if there is collusion or worse. My company does not intend to pay a half million dollars in double indemnity for a death clearly not an accident."

The sheriff sat staring at her for another minute without speaking. Finally, he stood up and said, "My report is final. I know nothing about Gloria's threats. I have only your hearsay, and your company has a half-million dollar motive to obscure the issue. You may leave now."

He walked to the door and held it open, glaring at her. Matilda walked to him and said, "I'm sorry you feel forced to conceal the facts. I will start a full investigation. Goodbye for now."

Matilda thanked the deputy and walked out. She felt an anxious prickling in her neck as she started her car, and became progressively more apprehensive as she drove out of town. She had just accused a man wearing a gun of being involved in a murder. He looked angry enough to do her harm. Oh dear!

Less than a mile down the road, Matilda pulled her Buick in between cars at the side of a diner. From a table near the front window, she ordered coffee and two muffins, and watched the traffic coming from town. Her apprehension slowly subsided as she made notes in her notepad, glancing up frequently to check the road. No sheriff's car passed, so she got back into her car and drove home, half expecting to see a flashing blue light in the rear view mirror. There was a lot to discuss with Hiram.

It seemed likely that Gloria Ingraham and Sheriff Darcy were involved in the death of Dr. Price. The sheriff's attitude confirmed many of her suspicions, even though he denied everything. Gloria's anger was understandable if she found Dr. Price caused the pregnancy of the sheriff's daughter. Maybe Dr. Price was the one who caused Gloria's pregnancy twenty years ago. That would make her motive even stronger. There were many loose ends, but further investigation would fill in the gaps, or blow a hole in her theory. Hiram could tell her what to do next.

Matilda decided to set the detective work aside for a while. Tonight was bridge night at Zelda's house. Tomorrow was soon enough to talk with Hiram. Matilda relaxed when she arrived home, knowing she made good progress today. The investigation was nearing a solution. She was sure that Gloria and Sheriff Darcy were the culprits. It was just a matter of finding out exactly how they did it.

CHAPTER SIX

Matilda Talks With Zelda

Matilda met Zelda for dinner before the evening of bridge. Zelda was pleased to see her old friend and mentor. After they placed their orders, Matilda asked how things were going at Doc's office. Zelda frowned, shook her head, and explained, "You and Doc asked me to assume your position of office manager. Both of you seemed sure that I could do it. Doc encouraged me, and gave me a good raise. There's no trouble with the billing and purchasing, but I'm not good at giving instructions. I try to give good leadership, but some of the staff seems to resent me. I know what needs to be done, and see when things aren't done the way Doc wants, but when I talk to them, they act as if I'm butting into their business. Maybe you could come back and be office manager, and let me just do the billing and bookkeeping."

Matilda smiled and reassured Zelda, "No. I've been there and done that. I'm finally where I want to be, a working detective. You're going to do fine."

"Maybe I will, but I don't know how to get their confidence."

"That takes time. You're only twenty-two, and the older staff are bound to resent Doc's promoting you over them. You can do it."

"I know you and Doc think so, but I don't know how. Can you give me any ideas?"

"I'll try. Let me describe a plan I've seen work. Tell me what you think of it. Tell Doc what you're planning. I'll help if it becomes necessary.

"OK. I need some kind of plan. Tell me how to do it."

"You've got to get them working with you, not against you. They need to feel as if the plan is theirs, not just yours."

"That sounds great, but how can I get them thinking that way?"

"You start by having half-hour meetings, one morning a week, with everyone there. Tell them it's part of their work, and they'll be paid for the time spent. At the first meeting, explain that Doc asked you to be office manager. Tell them you need all their help to do what he asked you to do. Ask them to help you make a list of goals for the staff. Get them to make suggestions for you to write on the blackboard. The goals should be broad, like *patient care* and *assisting Doc* and *a friendly office.* They may give some narrow suggestions. Write them all down, and then ask if some of them fit together. When everyone agrees upon a list of broad goals that is reasonable, let them think about them for a week. At the next meeting, write each goal on the board, one at a time. Then ask for ways to accomplish the listed goal. List their suggestions under the goal. Do one goal after another until all are covered. Take as many meetings as you need. When you complete this exercise, the list of goals and objectives is the work of the group. With goals and objectives in writing, and everyone agreeing what needs to be done, and how to do it, your job will be much easier."

Zelda listened and then said, "That's a plan. I can try it. What if someone wants to complain about something, and ties up the meeting?"

Matilda smiled, "I know who you have in mind. At the start, tell everyone that you will listen to any complaints or comments, but that will be done in your office, and not at the planning meeting. If Martha isn't cooperative, stop her, and pleasantly ask her to talk with you after the meeting is over."

Zelda said, "Martha never agrees to anything. I doubt she'll even agree that it's their job to help Doc and the patients."

Matilda nodded, "She can be difficult. She knew I wouldn't listen to her gripes, so she only complained to the others. You may have to replace her."

Zelda sat back and opened her eyes wide, asking, "You mean, have Doc fire Martha?"

"Talk to her alone first. Let her know you need her help. If she isn't willing to cooperate, that's the only way out. You must have people who will listen to you, and make the office work for Doc."

"I'll try that. I don't know if I could get someone fired."

"You can do whatever you have to do. Doc needs a well-run office, and you can do it. He has confidence in you. Let's have dinner together every week before bridge. You can let me know how it's going. I'll do anything I can to help, except go back and work at the office."

The waitress came with their meals as Zelda said, "OK, I'll try."

As they ate, the conversation turned to bridge. Zelda said, "I still don't know what some of the women mean by their bids. They all seemed to mean something different. How do you decide what they mean when they bid?"

Matilda smiled, "They're all good at playing the hands, but they don't use any bidding conventions except the most basic ones, Gerber and Blackwood. They don't even use Stayman, and may open a four card major. It's mostly guesswork as you change partners after each four hands. After a while, you know that this one overbids, and that one underbids, but it's not very scientific."

"You're right. I studied the Goren and Culbertson books you gave me. Maybe if they read the same books, they would bid better."

Matilda smiled, "They aren't going to change. I just relax and enjoy the company."

"I can do that. I do enjoy the group. But, tell me, you and David do well in national competition. You mentioned Precision bidding once. How do you do that?"

"That's different. In competition, we keep the same partner. Many pairs use complicated conventions. A few years ago, the Chinese developed a bidding system they called Precision. David wanted to learn it, so we practiced together. The bids all have definite meanings. For instance, with any hand having sixteen or more high card points, I open by bidding One Club. My partner's response indicates his point count, within a very narrow range. Knowing the point count in the two hands lets us know how high to bid. Then, it's just a matter of finding the best suit."

"It sounds complicated. Does it work for you?"

"Oh, yes. We do quite well. After learning the system, it's easy to bid, almost automatic. The partners know exactly what each bid means. We rarely overbid or underbid, and almost always end up in the right contract."

"Maybe I should learn it. It would be nice to know what every bid means."

Matilda shook her head, "It only works if both partners know the entire system. It would confuse the women we play with. If you find a partner to play with all the time, and want to learn Precision, it's not difficult. I'll lend you the book by Dr. Wei. It won't help in playing party bridge, but if you find a partner who wants to learn precision, you could go to some duplicate bridge clubs and use it."

"Maybe sometime. You haven't told me how your detective work is going. Are you solving cases?"

Matilda told her all about the investigation, concluding, "So, you see, I've found the murderers. We only need to get the police involved to wrap it up."

Zelda frowned, "I remember two years ago when you thought we'd solved the murder of Bryce's first wife. The two CID men left us feeling foolish. We thought we had all the answers and a complete case, but they shot holes in all our theories. Shouldn't you have more solid evidence before you involve them again?"

Matilda sat back, chagrinned. She recalled the two of them doing an amateur investigation of Zelda's husband. They had jumped to conclusions then, and that could be the case now. There were few facts, and she was jumping to conclusions again. The CID detectives would laugh at her. She admitted, "You're right, Zelda. Thanks for keeping the egg off my face. My conclusions are way ahead of the facts. I'm sure it was Gloria, and I know the Sheriff is involved, but I'll discuss everything with Hiram. He'll know what to do next."

"You're lucky to have him as a teacher. Is he as odd as he sounded on the phone?"

"Not really. Some of it is an act. He's not as backward as he wants everyone to believe. He's very bright, and I think well educated. I don't know him very well yet, but I really like him."

Zelda looked around the restaurant and chuckled, "Be careful where you say that. Handsome Harry will be after him. He's jealous of anybody who looks at you."

"I can take care of Harry. Let's go. It's time to go play bridge."

The two friends were a little distracted as they spent the evening playing bridge. Matilda knew she was pushing Zelda into an uncomfortable role, but Doc needed good help. Zelda wanted to go to college, and Matilda would help her do that, eventually. There was a lot of time for Zelda to get her education, but it was now or never to become a detective. She easily suppressed the temporary pang of guilt.

Zelda thought about the meetings, and how she could get the office staff organized as Matilda suggested. At least it was something to try. Matilda always helped her in so many ways. It was selfish to think of leaving Doc to go to college now, but maybe next year she could enroll in the University of Maine, after Matilda became a detective.

Neither one was near the top when the scores were added at the end of the evening.

CHAPTER SEVEN

Matilda Talks with Hiram

Matilda drove up the rutted Picked Mountain Road at eight the next morning. The sun was just peeking over the cliff behind the log cabin. Hiram again welcomed her at the door, and boomed, "Did you get the goods on him? Do we have the proof we need to put him away?"

Matilda walked in smiling. Hiram looked different, cleanly shaved and wearing a starched broadcloth shirt and ironed trousers. He was standing more erect and limping less. The change into a carefully groomed man was not lost on Matilda.

Matilda started, "I have a lot to tell you. The case isn't solved conclusively, but I think you'll be impressed with my progress. I'm ready for a cup of tea while I assemble my notes."

"The kettle's hot. I'll start it brewing. Tell me what proof you have."

Matilda sat at the table and opened her notebook. "It'll be better if I start at the beginning. That's what Doc liked and it's easier for me. You can help by telling me how I might have done differently."

Hiram grumbled, "Advice after action is like rain after the harvest. Do it however you want. What's time to a hog? We've got all day if you need it."

Matilda consulted her notebook and gave a detailed description of her activities, starting with her trip to Dr. Galliano's office and her discussions with Florence Gifford. She continued with the visit to Mrs. Price, the trip to

Greenville and her talk with Sheriff Darcy. Hiram made a few comments under his breath, but mostly listened with narrowed eyes and a frown. When she finished, he asked, "How do you know this State Health Nurse, Gloria Ingraham? She sounds like a bear. You make her out to be the murderer, or at least an accomplice. How is she involved in this case?"

"I know her very well. She's an effective State Health Nurse, but is a vindictive soul who enjoys punishing anyone who gets a venereal disease. According to the story I've heard from enough sources to believe it's true, she was seduced and impregnated by a surgeon when she was a young OR nurse. She gave the baby up for adoption and grew massively obese. The wags say that's why she feels good about punishing any man who has sex outside marriage. There's a possibility Dr. Price was the surgeon who seduced her a number of years ago. If he also seduced Sheriff Darcy's daughter, and threw her over, Gloria might feel justified in avenging the girl's death with murder. As I told you, she talked with Sheriff Darcy before, and after, Dr. Price died. If he feels Dr. Price caused his daughter's death, that may be why he's covering up a murder and calling it an accident. On the other hand, he might have done it himself."

Hiram listened and decided Matilda was a big help, even though it made him doubt his original convictions. He said, "Hells bells. You rule out one suspect and find two more. I haven't forgotten Dr, Galliano, but your theory does hold together better than mine. I may get my bonus yet."

Matilda smiled and asked, "What's next on our agenda? What do you suggest I do next?"

"We have to involve the police at some point, but I've found it's best to have all the answers before bringing them in. Sometimes they're too heavy handed to get the answers, and other times the legal restrictions slow them down. No police officer could have made the accusations you threw at Sheriff Darcy yesterday. Let's wait on that."

Matilda agreed, "I know we don't have hard facts yet. I wonder if I should see Gloria Ingraham and ask some questions. I know her well enough to tell if she's lying. If I tell her I've talked with Sheriff Darcy, and he told me about meeting her and discussing his daughter's problem, I may get more information."

Hiram became stern, "You might get yourself killed, too. Confronting a murderer is always risky. If she's killed once, she may feel no compunction about killing again. I lost one partner and don't ever want to lose another."

Matilda saw his frown and assured him, "I'll be careful."

She then hesitated and asked, "Or, do you have a better idea?"

"No. You talk with her. Just be careful. I'll do the research on the death of Sheriff Darcy's daughter. The newspapers will have her name and probably what she did for work. You said her picture showed her in a nurse's cap. If she was an OR nurse, or had other contact with Dr. Price, that will fit in with your theory. Questioning the people where she worked might fill in the gaps. That must be done very carefully. The people who think they got away with murder will start covering their tracks if they think a hound is on their trail. You've stirred the pot enough already with your accusations."

"I'm not always pushy. I'll do the legwork if you want. I'm younger than you."

Hiram bristled, "I may look like a cripple, but I get around all right. I'll do that part of the investigation. The spirit's willing, and the flesh is strong enough for that."

Matilda smiled and said, "OK. I just thought I'd offer. If you can tie her to Dr. Price, that will solidify our case. I know Sheriff Darcy called Gloria to help his daughter. It didn't work, but they are certainly in this together. I don't have proof, but I think Gloria did it, don't you?"

Hiram agreed, "You could be right. She's one obvious suspect at this time, but don't count your chickens before the eggs are hatched."

"Then you think contacting Gloria is my next assignment?"

"Yes, but be very careful. I am getting used to having an apprentice. I don't want to lose you. From small beginnings come great things. Use the phone and see if you can set up an appointment. I need to know when and where before you meet her."

Matilda called the familiar number. The State Health office said Gloria was not there, but planned to be in Lakewood the next day. They made an appointment for Gloria to come to Matilda's new office at nine the next morning.

That reminded Matilda about her sign and business cards. She asked Hiram, "What should my business cards say? I need to be able to give people my number. I should have some title. Exactly what am I?"

"You're neither fish nor fowl. I called the Maine Licensing Board. You have to make an application, and get them to approve it, before you can be a licensed apprentice to Murphy Investigations. That's the name I put on my bills. They're sending me the paperwork. They said you could work with me investigating a claim for the insurance company, even before your license comes. Investigating for an insurance company is an exception to the private investigator law."

"Do you think I can get some cards printed now, with my name and Murphy Investigations on it? Can I get a sign painted saying Murphy Investigations?"

"When you get your license, it'll be OK if you use that name, with your name and address under it. You may want to choose a different name for yourself in a year, or we could continue working together. I'd like you to consider that."

"I'm sure they'll give me a license. I'll get the business cards printed. I think I'll have them finish the sign, too. As an apprentice, can I call myself a private investigator? I mean, can the sign read: MURPHY INVESTIGATIONS, Matilda Parker, P. I.? Maybe you'd like your name on it, also? You could use my office any time you need a more formal place to meet someone. I like the idea of making the sign read like this:"

Matilda drew a sign on her notepad:

MURPHY INVESTIGATIONS
Hiram Murphy, P.I.
Matilda Parker, P.I.

Hiram looked at it and scowled for a while. Matilda began to wonder if she was pushing too hard, but finally he said thoughtfully, "It's OK. It's a common name. I've been out of sight long enough. I don't intend to work very hard. If it suits you, go ahead. We'll make a willing team. You're willing to work and I'm willing to let you."

"I'll put my telephone number on my business cards. Do you want me to have some made for you?"

Hiram thought for another minute before answering, "Yeah, mine are about gone. You could make them with both names and both telephone numbers, and use your address. I don't think anyone would confuse one of us for the other. Even with a hat on, a horse is still a horse."

"I'll do that. Oh, is there anything else I need to know about getting licensed?"

"There is one other thing. You're going to need a permit to carry a concealed weapon. You have to go to the town office for that. How are you with a pistol? Are you a good shot?"

"Good lord, no! I've never fired a gun. My father hated guns. Do I really have to fire one?"

Hiram smiled, "It's about time you learned. You probably won't ever need it, but it's a requirement for getting a PI license. They've talked about eliminating that part of the law, but for now, it's something you have to do. You have to pass a test to be sure you know how to fire it accurately, and understand the restrictions on its use."

"Can you teach me? I know nothing about guns."

"Sure. I have a pistol range out back. Actually, you won't have to carry a weapon, if you don't want to. The law says you have to have the handgun permit, and know how to use one, but there's no requirement to carry or even own one, after you pass the test."

"Then we can use yours for practice?"

"We could, but mine's too big for you. I'll pick up a little twenty-two for you to use. I can always use it for varmints or plinking. It'll meet the requirements, and you can handle it easily. We'll get to that next week."

Matilda was doubtful, but then said, "Then back to detective work. I think Gloria could give us the answers, if she will. She's so self-righteous that she may give herself away. I have a plan for nine tomorrow morning. I'll let you know what I find out."

"That's good, Matilda. I'll drive into Portland this afternoon. I went to school with the nurse who's been OR supervisor at MMC for fifteen years. I think she'll let us know if the Darcy woman worked there. She may even know if Dr. Price was the one who got Gloria pregnant. What are your plans for the rest of today?"

"My next stop is at the printing office and then to the sign painter. I'm eager to get the accoutrements of a real private investigator. You don't know how many years I've thought about it, and now it's almost a reality. My thanks to you for that."

"You better wait to thank me. It's not all roses. Only a new kettle is shiny"

"The shine may wear off, but I'm excited about what we're doing now. I'll let you know if I ever get bored. Right now I'm learning every day."

"If you're successful, I won't stand in your light. Now, off with you. Let's talk tomorrow after you've seen Gloria."

"And after you've found out if Ms. Darcy worked in the hospital."

Matilda drove down the mountain road feeling good about herself. The meeting with Gloria tomorrow should get the answers they needed.

At her office, Matilda typed a summary of the case, listing the few known facts and the multiple suppositions. There were still more questions than answers. Keeping a written record of everything she did made sense to her, and would make it easier to discuss ideas with Hiram. Having all the data correlated also would make it easier to present the case to the CID detectives, when the time came for that. There were many holes in the story. At the end of her typed report, she listed questions needing answers. She hoped Gloria would provide more facts in the morning.

CHAPTER EIGHT

Matilda Asks Gloria

Gloria was prompt, knocking on Matilda's door at exactly nine AM. She had a sour expression and followed Matilda into the new office without speaking. They sat, and Matilda smiled as she said, "Good morning, Gloria. Thank you for coming."

"You're not welcome. I came to set the record straight. Sheriff Darcy called me. He said you accused him of aiding me in killing Dr. Price. I knew you were a busybody but I didn't think you were a dreamer. Such an accusation could land you in jail for defamation of character. You just repeat that absurd accusation and I'll be pleased to press charges and see you rot in jail."

Matilda kept smiling and said, "It's good to have all the cards on the table, Gloria. The sheriff said you talked with him about the death of his daughter before Dr. Price was murdered, and several times afterwards. With your animosity against Dr. Price for what he did to you, I'm not surprised that you felt he didn't deserve to live, after doing the same thing to the Darcy girl."

Gloria sat and stared at Matilda for a minute before speaking. She gaped twice then said, "You are assuming a lot of facts not in evidence, as the lawyers say. You must believe everything you've heard about me."

"Yes, I know what happened to you. Until now, I didn't know it was Dr. Price. He ruined a lot of lives, preying on young women, leading them on, and then discarding them."

"You don't know the half of it. More than a dozen of his offspring have gone through the adoption program, and dozens more were aborted. He's been a menace to society for two decades, but that doesn't prove anything. I'm glad he's dead. The world is better off without that lecher alive to ruin the lives of young women."

"His actions were reprehensible. That still doesn't excuse what you did. I can understand Sheriff Darcy covering for you, and calling it an accident, even though that explanation doesn't fit the facts and makes no sense. The loss of his daughter is a tragedy. I feel badly for him. He's still suffering. You've suffered long enough. It's time to clear your conscience and get it behind you."

Gloria stiffened, "You'd like that, wouldn't you. You'd like a confession so I could spend the rest of my life in the company of all the people I've put in jail. Well, it won't happen. I haven't done anything that I'm not proud of. Somebody killed the bastard, but you can't prove it was me."

"I can and I will. There is never an adequate excuse for murder."

Gloria pushed her bulk out of the chair and stared at Matilda before stalking out of the room without saying anything else. She slammed the door hard enough to make the windows rattle. Matilda sat there, wondering how she might have handled the interview better. It was clear that Gloria hated Dr. Price. She as much as admitted he was the one who got her pregnant. She also agreed that he was murdered, although she denied doing it.

Matilda was sure she knew the murderer, just as Hiram had been, but he was wrong. Could there be another explanation? Was Gloria covering for Darcy, or was Darcy covering for Gloria? They were not the only ones Dr. Price had injured. Unless Hiram had other ideas, it seemed time to talk to the police who could use their methods of investigating. The police could get Gloria's schedule and know where she was on September fifteenth when Dr. Price was killed. They could get Sheriff Darcy's schedule, do a better examination of the hunting lodge, and check for fingerprints. Exhuming the body was a possibility. There was a lot to discuss with Hiram this afternoon. For now, her calling cards were at the printers, and the sign should be ready. There were many things for a detective to do besides detect.

Matilda was hanging the new sign on the post when Harry Darling stopped and walked over, smiling. "So you did it."

He looked at the sign and frowned, "Who is Hiram Murphy?"

"Hi, Harry. Hiram is a retired police detective, now a licensed private investigator. I'm his apprentice for a year. We're working together on a case. How are you doing?"

"I'm fine. Can I help you with that sign?"

"I think it's all hung. Is it straight? How do you think it looks?"

"It looks good. Tell me about Hiram. How old is he?"

Matilda smiled, "He's much too old for me, if that's what's bothering you. He lives alone on Picked Mountain. He's an interesting character and teaching me a lot. Would you like to see my new office?"

"Sure. You're really going through with this. I hoped it was just a passing fancy, but now I see how serious you are. I'd like to see your office. If there's anything I can do to help, you only have to ask."

They went into Zelda's office and sat in the new leather chairs. Harry was impressed as he looked around. The office had a professional look. He said, "I like it. Can you tell me about the case you're working on, or is that a professional secret?"

"Most of what we know is public knowledge. The name of our client isn't important. We're investigating the death of Dr. Price in his hunting camp in Greenville last September fifteenth. The local sheriff called it an accident, but really it was murder. We've identified the prime suspect. This afternoon, we'll decide when to bring in the police to complete the investigation and make the arrest. I'm really enjoying the work."

"You think an accident was really a murder? Why do you think the sheriff made a mistake like that? I know Sheriff Darcy. He's a good man."

"We think he was involved. You know his daughter committed suicide. The doctor who died was responsible for her actions. Sheriff Darcy was in frequent contact with the perpetrator. He probably isn't the murderer, but he seems to be covering for the one who is."

"Those are all suppositions. If you have hard evidence, you need to get the police involved right now. If it involves a county sheriff, the State Police CID and the Attorney General's office need to be informed. You shouldn't withhold evidence of a murder."

"That's the problem. We don't have any hard evidence. It's all circumstantial. I'll talk with Hiram this afternoon. If he agrees, we'll give everything we have to the proper officials. He's in charge. I just collect information and develop theories."

"The sooner you contact the CID, the better. Even with strong suspicion, you should get them involved. Evidence disappears quickly as time goes by."

"I understand. I'll talk with Hiram. It seems to me it's time to get them involved. Thanks for your advice. I'll let you know what we decide to do."

"Great. Stay in touch. I hope you have this wrapped up before Christmas. Steamboat Springs has a good package for the holidays to attract the college students."

"I'll have to see what my boss says. He said he had another insurance case that he hasn't told me about yet. Don't make any plans without talking with me first."

CHAPTER NINE

Matilda Makes Plans

Hiram related his discoveries first. Betty Darcy worked as an OR nurse at the hospital. That was why Gloria identified with her. Her situation was similar to Gloria's experience fifteen years earlier. Betty told her friends she was planning to get married, and left her job without notice. They were devastated when news of her suicide reached them. They described her as cheerful and upbeat, making her suicide almost unbelievable. No one had any idea why she did it.

Matilda gave him a copy of her typed notes, which he glanced at and set aside, saying, "I'm glad to have someone else do the paperwork. I always wanted everything right, so I put off writing anything until the end. No report of mine ever had a misspelled word. Lazy folk take the most pains."

Matilda smiled and described her meeting with Gloria, including her tacit admission that Dr. Price was murdered, although she denied being the culprit. They reviewed all the data they had. There were two more possible murderers, Gloria and Sheriff Darcy, with Gloria being the most likely one. Hiram reluctantly agreed that Dr. Galliano was not the prime suspect, although he was the only one with real financial gain. He said, "Money talks and sometimes uses big words. When someone is murdered, if it's not the husband or wife, the most likely culprit is the one who gets the money."

Several young women had reason to wish Dr. Price harm, but no other names came up. It seemed certain that

Gloria and Sheriff Darcy knew what happened. Hiram stared out the window without speaking for quite a while, and then said, "We really don't have enough to talk with the State Police CID detectives. When a law enforcement officer is accused of a crime, it's never easy to get an investigation. They hate to believe one of their own is on the wrong side of the fence. Maybe your State Police Sergeant friend will be able to steer us in the right direction."

"Harry will do anything he can to help us, when the time comes. I know two of the State Police CID detectives. They investigated another case I had. They proved that he was guilty. Whenever you think it's time, I'll ask Harry to have them get in touch with us."

Hiram thought briefly before answering, "Let's go over your notes and review where we are and what we know. You assume that Dr. Galliano has Parkinson's disease, but you haven't met him. Perhaps you should."

"Florence, his office nurse, agreed that he had the signs and symptoms of Parkinson's. I think that's probably correct. On the other hand, you were convinced he was the murderer after you talked with him, and he did get the money. I'd be glad to meet him and make my own assessment, if you think that might help."

"It wouldn't hurt. We need to tie up some loose ends. Right now, we're neither here nor there. You said Dr. Price's wife told you all the assets and liabilities of the practice reverted to the surviving partner. That's like a tontine agreement. With the delay in insurance claim payments to doctors, and the large amount usually in accounts receivable, that must have been another big boost to Dr. Galliano's pocketbook. He can tell you about that, if you approach him right. Florence must know about that too. I'm surprised she didn't know about the mutual insurance policies."

"I was surprised, too. I ran the office for two doctors, and I'd certainly know about anything like that. I'll talk with her again. She seemed honest and open, but she could be covering up something. I'll try to see her the same day I see Dr. Galliano."

"That's good. When I checked the papers for the Darcy girl's name, I also found the names of the two men who came to hunt with Dr. Price. I'll call them and try to find out exactly what they saw. The deputy seemed totally incompetent and fouled up the scene, but those men might have noticed something important."

"The deputy seemed willing to talk with me. He told me about Darcy's daughter. I might be able to get some more information from him. It means another trip to Greenville, but it might give us some answers."

"You do that. We're a long way from involving the State CID. Oh. When you go to Greenville, you might get the keys to the hunting camp from Mrs. Price. It's not considered a crime scene so you could legally look around. There may be some solid clue there. Lord knows we could use something concrete."

"Things like Gloria's schedule and Sheriff Darcy's activities are beyond our abilities to determine now. Those answers will have to wait for the CID."

"You might get some information from the deputy. He acted like his elevator didn't get to the top floor, but he might have log, even if he can't remember."

"Let's get together again in two days. I'll call if anything seems urgent."

Hiram started to stand, then sat again and asked, "You said you had a prior case. Tell me about that. I thought being a detective was new to you. What aren't you telling me?"

"Oh, that. Doc is a medical examiner. I helped him with some of the cases he investigated. I was an amateur then, but with your help, I'll become more professional. I'll tell you about it sometime, but now we have a lot to do. Harry said evidence disappears rapidly. I was thinking, the cabin should be checked for fingerprints, if it hasn't already been done. Is that something you can do?"

"Oh, I could lift the fingerprints, but I'd have nothing to compare them with. What a person doesn't have in his mind has to be made up with his feet. We'll have to do more legwork."

"OK, legwork it is. You mentioned another insurance case. Is there anything I can do to help there?"

Hiram walked around and looked out all the windows, before he came back and answered, "There is a lot to do in that case. I talked with the people and got nowhere. I backed off because I thought Mr. Calzoni might recognize me. It was his house that was robbed. I probably should tell you, there are people in New Jersey who wanted me dead and thought they had killed me. I was in intensive care for four weeks. When I started to recover, the commissioner told everyone that I died, then put me in a hearse and brought me here. Doc and a couple people on the force know I'm alive, and even they don't know where I am. There are Calzonis in the mob. Richard Calzoni may have no connection, but he started looking at me funny when I talked with him. I don't think he bought my Maine twang and colorful language."

"So that's why you're so nervous. This place is like a fort. No one could get up the mountain without you knowing it. Wait a minute. I heard the Calzoni name before. When I asked the deputy if Dr. Galliano had talked with him, he said I had the name wrong. He had written down the name of Calzoni. There may be more Calzonis living in Maine. I don't know what that means, if anything."

"I don't either, but I'll let you do the traveling and investigating. You be careful, though. They're not after you, but they aren't choosy who they kill if you're in the way."

Sure, I'll do the investigating. I don't have to fake being a Mainer."

"I worried about that for a while, but you're right. No one will suspect you. I do need to stay in the background. For now, let's see if we can get the answers on Dr. Price's death. The robbery can wait."

"Fine, I'll see you in a couple days."

"One more thing. I picked up the twenty-two. You need the serial number to get the permit. Take this receipt to the town office. They'll give you the permit."

"It seems like a waste of time, but I'll do it. I'll do whatever it takes to get my license, even learn to fire a gun."

"We'll get to that later. For now, let's get some facts."

CHAPTER TEN

Matilda Asks Dr. Galliano

Matilda decided to go to Portland first. She wanted to verify the diagnosis of Parkinson's disease. It seemed logical, and Florence Gifford agreed the symptoms matched the diagnosis. It was surprising that Florence didn't recognize it earlier. She said she thought he might be ill, and noticed he was slowing down. She must have questioned the change in operating schedules. Maybe she wasn't as truthful as she appeared. Not knowing about the partnership agreements was more questionable. Matilda decided to be more aggressive in her interview today. Florence was in the office from eight to noon. That was the place to start.

Matilda didn't call ahead, but just went to the back door of the office and knocked. Florence opened the door and acted startled as she recognized Matilda. She stood in the doorway and hesitated before asking, "What can I do for you today, Matilda?"

"The insurance company asked me to obtain additional information. May I come in?"

Florence hesitated again, and said, "Now is not a good time. Can you come back tomorrow?"

Matilda smiled pleasantly as she asked, "How about later this morning. I have another errand and could come back about eleven if that would be acceptable."

Florence thought briefly before agreeing, "Eleven will be all right. I'll see you then."

Matilda walked to her car and looked around. A large man was leaning on a stretch Mercedes parked in the space beside the building marked "Doctors Only". He saw her and frowned. She smiled, waved, got into her car and drove away. Probably Dr. Galliano was in the office. That was not surprising. There are many details involved in closing a practice; finalizing payroll and taxes, paying bills, collecting accounts receivable, selling equipment, and maybe the office building. It was all his now. He must be working with Florence. It was curious that she did not want Matilda to see them together. There was more to the arrangement than just an office manager and her boss.

Matilda drove slowly toward Cape Elizabeth with a plan forming in her mind. If things worked well, she could watch Dr. Galliano walk and confirm the suspected diagnosis. Then she'd try to talk to him. He wouldn't be expecting her and might provide more information than with a scheduled visit. She stopped in a small shopping mall on Shore Road and parked where she could easily move out into traffic. She was becoming restless and wondered about her plan when the Mercedes from Dr. Galliano's office drove past. She eased into traffic and followed it at a safe distance. When it turned into a circular driveway and stopped in front of a large house, she parked across the street. She watched the big man help Dr. Galliano out of the car and assist him as he shuffled into the house. After the door closed, Matilda drove up behind the Mercedes and parked. She walked up to the door and rang the bell. There was no response for more than a minute, so she rang the bell again. The butler appeared and partially opened the door. He narrowed his eyes and said, "You! I saw you at the office. What do you want?"

"It's important that I talk with Dr, Galliano. The Underwriters want this claim settled as soon as possible. May I see him now?"

The butler was firm, "He's resting now. Perhaps if you call for an appointment, it can be arranged."

Matilda became serious and said, "You should ask Dr. Galliano. Here is my card. The Bell Underwriters claim will not be processed until I get the answers they requested. A delay now could take months to correct. If I can't see him now, I will return in a month or two. I have other things to do besides wait for him to decide to see me."

The butler stood for a minute before he said, "Wait here."

Matilda stood on the step for less than a minute before the door opened again and the butler said pleasantly, "Please come in, Ms. Parker. Dr. Galliano will be pleased to see you now."

"Thank you."

Matilda was ushered through a wide foyer into a beautiful living room with large windows looking out onto Casco Bay. Dr. Galliano sat in a recliner and managed a smile as he asked her to take a chair opposite him. He talked slowly and carefully, "I gave all the information to your associate. The policy seemed straightforward when the agent sold it to us. We filed a legitimate claim, but the company is balking at paying. Do I need a lawyer?"

"Not necessarily. Most similar claims are settled promptly without involving a lawyer. It depends upon how long it takes to get the answers to some questions. The company must protect its investors."

"I understand. Ask whatever questions you have. I'll be pleased to provide all the answers in whatever detail you need. It is important to me to have this settled as soon as possible."

Matilda put her new tape recorder on the table, started it, then opened a notebook and studied it, briefly. She looked at Dr. Galliano and asked, "Do you mind if I record your answers, Dr. Saul Galliano. It helps me make my report more accurate."

"Not at all. What questions do you need answered?"

She glanced at her notebook again and then asked, "When did you become disabled with Parkinson's Disease, Dr. Galliano?"

The doctor sat quietly for a long time without changing his expression. Finally, he said, "I'm not yet disabled, although it will not be long before I am. Why is this important to the insurance company?"

Matilda glanced at her notebook, and said, "I'm not sure why these questions are important, but the underwriters need the answers. Are you aware of a claim being filed for payment of the policy because of your disability?"

Again, Dr. Galliano waited a long time before answering, "I'm sure such a claim was never filed. Whereas I'm not disabled, such a claim would be unfounded. Dr. Price and I discussed everything. I would know if he even thought about filing a claim."

Matilda watched his face carefully. Hiram was right. There was no way to determine his emotions from his expressions or his voice. His face was a mask. She made a note in her notebook, and said, "The Company needs the name of your treating physician, and a signed release for your medical file. I have the release form here for your signature."

As he stared at her without answering, the front door slammed and Florence Gifford rushed into the room and hurried to his side saying breathlessly, "Jason called me, Saul. You don't need to say anything."

Dr. Galliano looked at her and said, "It's all right, Florence. I can answer all her questions. Have a seat. I'll handle this."

"But you don't know. I need to talk with you."

Dr. Galliano took her hand and reassured her, "Just go sit down, Florence. She has only a few questions and I've answered most of them. If she has questions for you, I'm sure you can answer them. It's important to get this cleared up as soon as possible. Please sit down and let Mrs. Parker complete her list of questions."

Florence wasn't convinced, but he looked at her calmly. Finally, she squeezed his hand, went slowly to a chair and sat on the edge of the seat.

As they talked, Matilda formulated a plan. It might only get denials, but should evoke some response. It seemed worth a try. Matilda continued, enunciating clearly, "Then, Dr. Galliano, you weren't aware that Dr. Price asked this lady, Ms Florence Gifford, to file a claim for payment of the policy based upon your disability?"

When Dr. Galliano hesitated, Florence jumped to her feet, stared at Matilda, and said, "How do you know about that. There's no way you could know. I didn't do it."

Dr. Galliano became agitated and leaned forward, sputtering, "What are you saying, Florence? He wouldn't do that to me. He said we'd continue the practice with me just seeing patients in the office and him doing all the surgery. You worked out the schedule. You know our arrangement."

She came over to take his hand and said, "He was leading you on, darling. He told me to do it. Oh, dear. I couldn't let that happen."

Dr. Galliano dropped her hand and stared at her. Finally, he said, "Tell me about it, Florence. What did you do?"

Florence knelt beside Dr. Galliano and took his hand again, ignoring everyone else in the room, saying, "I talked to him, but he wouldn't listen. I went to his cabin and pleaded with him. I knew how much that insurance meant to you. He just laughed at me. He even laughed when I picked up his shotgun. He said, 'It isn't loaded," and showed me the clip he had removed.

He kept smiling and said, "Just be reasonable, Florence. Put the shotgun down and we'll talk."

I pushed it against his chest and told him, 'I wish it was loaded. I'd pull the trigger like this', and the gun went off."

Dr. Galliano stared at her and said, "My God. You killed him."

"I didn't mean to. It was an accident. I just wanted to scare him. He said the gun wasn't loaded so I pulled the trigger. I didn't mean to kill him."

They stared at each other silently, Dr Galliano incredulous, and Florence in extreme distress. Matilda broke the silence, "That's all my questions. I think the company has enough information to pay the claim. Whether they will call it an accident or something else is up to them."

They both looked at Matilda as she folded up her notebook, turned off the tape recorder, and rose from her chair. Dr. Galliano asked, "What do we do now?"

Matilda said, "I've completed my work. All the questions were answered. You don't need a lawyer, Dr.

Galliano, but Florence will need a good one. I think you should call one now. I believe the lawyer will advise you to call the police and give them a full accounting of what happened. If there's no attempt to cover up the facts, they may agree that it was an accident. Now that all four of us know what happened and why, there's nothing to hide."

Dr. Galliano's face didn't change expression, but he said loudly, "Wait! What about the insurance claim?"

Matilda said, "I don't know. That's up to the company. Good day."

She walked out with Dr. Galliano and Florence staring at each other, but not speaking. The butler brought a telephone and placed it beside Dr. Galliano's chair.

CHAPTER ELEVEN

Case Solved

Driving home, Matilda kept breaking into a smile as she thought about the case. Hiram would get his bonus. She was a real detective, at least a real apprentice. Now she could call herself a detective without any hesitation or reservation. Doc and Zelda would be proud of her. Life was great.

Her elation faded as she thought about Sheriff Darcy and Gloria. Zelda admonished her about jumping to unwarranted conclusions. She winced, thinking of her presumptuous accusations, and resolved never to do that again. Probably Gloria and Sheriff Darcy knew nothing about what happened, or maybe they did. Either way, there was no evidence that they were involved. Their pleasure at Dr. Price's demise was real and obvious. Unless Florence Gifford implicated them, they were in the clear.

Matilda tried to imagine what the insurance company would make of the developments. They might call it an accidental death, and pay Dr. Galliano the double indemnity. They might try to locate the letter Dr. Price asked Florence to send them, calling Dr. Galliano disabled. If it were legally binding, they might pay Dr. Price's estate the face amount, and pay Dr. Galliano nothing. That was for someone else to decide.

Dr. Galliano would probably get the value of the practice in any case. He had witnesses to prove that he had no involvement in Dr. Price's death. However, the letter saying he was disabled, if it existed, could mean the assets of the practice belonged to Dr. Price's widow. There was a lot for the lawyers to sort out. Her advice to Dr. Galliano, about not needing a lawyer, may have been wrong.

Florence was in real trouble. She was holding the shotgun that killed Dr. Price, whether she intended to kill him or not. She was angry and had strong reasons to protect Dr. Galliano. Her lawyer would have trouble convincing a jury that it was an accident.

The case was solved, but the wrangling by the lawyers might take years. That was not her problem. She sped along, eager to tell Hiram how well Matilda, the detective, had done. She forgot about lunch and sped up the winding road to Hiram's cabin. He met her at the door, saying, "I heard you coming. Haste makes waste."

Matilda smiled, "I've got news, good news."

"You look like the cat that swallowed the canary. Pride goes before a fall. Come in and sit down. I've some news for you. Would you like a cup of tea? It's hot."

Matilda sat and smiled, willing to relish her triumph in leisure. "I'd like that. Tell me your news first, and then I'll tell you mine."

Hiram brought the cups, poured the tea, sat down and said, "I phoned both the men who discovered Dr. Price's body. They called the Sheriff's Office as soon as they found him. When the Deputy came, they told him that the door was unlocked, and they thought he'd been murdered, but the Deputy told them it was an accident, and they could stay for the night. He didn't even suggest that they not clean up the place. They told me the deputy must not watch detective stories on the TV, or he'd know better. They corroborated my conviction that the Deputy Sheriff is totally incompetent. All the evidence at the scene is probably gone."

Matilda sipped her tea and smiled, "I'm sure your right. Would you like to hear what I found out?"

Hiram stroked his chin and said, "I'd better listen before you explode. Tell me your story."

Matilda told him of the situation leading up to the confession, and played the tape so he could hear Florence's words exactly as she said them. Hiram sat quietly without commenting until she finished. Then he said, "Damn. That's good work. We were both wrong in our assumptions. Confession is good for the soul, and it helped solve this case. You said there were three witnesses to that taped confession?"

Matilda beamed at the compliment, "Yes, besides me, there was Dr. Galliano and his caretaker in the room. No one has any reason to lie or deny it, as far as I know. I told them to call the police and let them know what happened. I also suggested that Florence get a good lawyer."

"She'll need one. For your information, the tape probably can't be used as evidence. You had Dr. Galliano's permission to tape the conversation, but you didn't get permission from Florence. The testimony of the witnesses is great, but a good lawyer will get the tape thrown out. The prosecution can use it to refresh the memory of the witnesses, but the jury probably won't be allowed to hear it. There's one more thing for you to do. No job is complete until the paperwork is done. I want you to type up a complete report on all our investigation and findings. The police will want it, and I need it for the insurance company. Make a copy for his brother. He'll be pleased to know it wasn't a careless accident."

"I can make a copy of the tape for them, too, if you think that's a good idea, or I can type that verbatim."

"That's a good idea. That's good evidence for the insurance company and his brother. Yes, make a couple copies of the tape, and type it also. Every nail in the coffin makes it that much stronger."

Matilda said, "I think I should re-write the notes I gave you earlier, covering our investigation and what we found."

Hiram said, "Right. You don't need to tell everyone that I was convinced that Dr. Galliano was the killer, or that you believed it was Gloria and Sheriff Darcy. It's probably a good idea to start the whole thing over. That's why I left the report to the last thing I did."

Matilda agreed, "Fine. I'll bring it back in the morning. Or, maybe you'd like to see our office. It has your name on the sign out front."

"Sounds like a plan. I think my jeep will make it down the mountain. I'll be there tomorrow morning about nine, if that's all right."

"I'm looking forward to it. With this case wrapped up so quickly, maybe we can talk about the other insurance case you mentioned."

"It's got me stumped. Maybe you can find the answers there as quickly as you did this time."

"I was lucky this time. I have a question. How did Florence kill him with an empty shotgun? If Dr. Price unloaded his shotgun and showed her the clip with the shells in it, how did it go off?"

"We'll get to a study of firearms soon. Most accidental deaths from firearms are caused by a weapon thought to be empty. He must have jacked one shell into the chamber sometime, and then forgot about it. Removing the clip doesn't get the shell out of the chamber. It had one round left in the shotgun, and that killed him."

"I guess I understand. Do you have a book on firearms? I learn a lot from books. There's nothing in my library to help me."

Hiram limped over to his desk, picked up a small book, and brought it to her, saying, "This is the basic text we used in New Jersey. It doesn't give you all the answers, but it's a good start. Study this, and we'll talk about it later. A little knowledge is a dangerous thing. There's enough information in the book to let you pass the test, but using a firearm is something else again."

"I hope I never have to use one, but I like to know as much as I can about things, so I understand when someone else uses one."

"I have some books on forensics. Those go into much more detail. We'll get to that during the next year. I learn best when there's a reason to know something. For now, study the basic book."

"Thanks, Hiram. I'll see you in the morning."

Hiram watched her go, feeling good about everything. The case was solved, and he had a lovely partner. His life was looking better than any time since his injury.

Matilda maneuvered the narrow road carefully. Solving the killing of Dr. Price was mostly luck. Having Hiram as a mentor was as good as it gets. Working with him was fun, and the thought of getting to know him better was exciting. He seemed attracted to her, and he was a very handsome man.

CHAPTER TWELVE

The Calzoni Case

Hiram rang the front doorbell at just 9 AM. Matilda opened the door and smiled at the change in Hiram's appearance. With a fresh haircut and cleanly shaved, wearing gray trousers and a blue sport coat with a Harvard necktie, he looked very professional. She said, "Good morning, Hiram. You look great. I recognize the tie. My father wore one like that when he wanted to impress someone. Did you graduate from Harvard?"

"A long time ago. I thought I wanted to be a lawyer, but found investigating crimes more up my alley. I've never regretted my choice. Lawyers have to do too many trade-offs. Winning a case becomes more important than finding the truth."

Matilda smiled, "We both thought we might become lawyers, and here we are, partners in finding the truth. Let me show you our office."

He followed her into the refurbished parlor, looked around the room, admired the furnishings; and then said, "This is a great office, Matilda. I like it. This is a big house. Have you lived here long?"

"All my life, so far. I spent three years in Portland, going to nursing school, and two more years in radiology training. Otherwise, this has been my home, ever since I was born. I've live alone since my parents died, except for a few months when Zelda, a good friend, lived here with me. Would you like me to show you around?"

Hiram said, "Yes. We have time. The Calzoni case has bugged me for six months. It can wait a little longer. Give me the grand tour."

Matilda took him outside and showed him the flower gardens and the new sign. They entered the barn, and walked through the shed connecting it to the house. As they talked, Matilda became amused. Hiram's language and manner had changed as much as his clothes. He now looked a professional investigator in every way. They went through the kitchen and dining room, into the library. Hiram was suitably impressed with the walls of reference books her father left her. He looked at the stacks of journals and asked, "This place looks used. Do you read all these magazines?"

"No. I flip through them when they come, and read some of the articles. A lot are too technical to be useful. I do get some ideas, and sometimes can remember where I saw the answer to a question when it comes up. My father had them bound and indexed at the end of each year. I still do that. That shelf over there has the bound copies of the four major journals. It's easier to find information after they're indexed."

"Impressive. You have a better library than we had at the station house. Would you mind if I spend some time here. I'd like to research a couple things."

"We're partners. You can spend as much time here as you want. I'll be glad to help you find things."

"That's great. I need all the help I can get. The old forget what the young haven't discovered. Show me the rest of the house, and I'll tell you about our other case."

They walked up the wide stairway and Matilda showed him the several bedrooms. He paused in the bedroom she said was hers, pushed his hand down on the firm mattress, and smiled as he asked, "Do you always sleep here alone?"

Matilda stopped and thought rapidly. Had she been turning him on? Was she being seductive? Nothing was more important than their professional relationship. After a brief pause, she said calmly, "Yes, in this house I sleep alone. I still feel my mother's presence here. In my family's house, I only entertain on the first floor."

Hiram nodded and followed her down the stairs. Matilda was eager to hear about his next case, so she kept walking and guided him back to the remodeled front parlor. They sat in the soft leather chairs as Matilda said, "OK, Hiram. Tell me what has you frustrated."

"Frustrated is a good word. Oh, you mean the case. Well, I'm stumped there, too. I'll tell you what I know. There was a robbery at the Calzoni estate six months ago. The thief only took jewelry, but there was enough of that to upset the insurance company. Virginia Calzoni had several very valuable pieces, left her by her grandmother. They were unique heirlooms, all appraised and photographed for the insurance company. The diamond and emerald necklace alone was valued at $175,000. The rest totaled about the same. The thief got away with a third of a million dollars worth of jewelry. Of course it's not worth that much to a fence, but Bell Underwriters had to pay the appraised value."

Matilda leaned forward and asked, "So where do you, or we, come in? Does the insurance company want us to investigate the theft?"

"Yeah, they contacted me four months ago. They have some suspicions about the loss. There was evidence of a break in, and there was evidence of someone escaping after being mauled by the dogs. The safe was left unlocked, according to the Calzonis. Virginia said she opened the safe earlier in the evening, took out her pearl earrings and necklace, but closed the door without latching it, thinking she might want to change her accessories before she left for the evening. She did not go back and latch the safe, so the thief opened it easily."

Matilda furrowed her brow, "I see why they're suspicious. That means there had to be two unrelated things that happened coincidentally. It takes a lot of credulity to believe the thief broke into the house on the only night the safe was left unlocked, and knew where to look."

"Right. Bell Underwriters told me they'd give me one third of the value of any jewelry I recovered, a handsome offer. I've tried, but I can't spin a thread. Every lead I've found has turned into a dead end. I don't believe the Calzoni's story, but I can't find any handles big enough to grab onto."

As Hiram talked, Matilda made quick notes on a pad on her desk. She thought for a minute, and then said, "I don't have a clear picture yet. You said the dogs mauled the thief. Tell me more about that."

"Yeah, that's one fly in the ointment. Two vicious Doberman Pinchers guard the Calzoni estate, inside a high fence. They are turned loose at night, and were loose the night the theft took place. It's hard to believe someone could get by them to get to the house, much less get away. I drove there in my jeep and they almost climbed in the window before I got close to the house. They bark at shadows and can run like greased lightning. On the night the jewels disappeared, the maid and butler were both in their quarters and didn't hear anything until they heard a commotion and the dogs barking. They turned on the lights and called the dogs. After a few minutes the dogs came. One had blood on his muzzle. The butler put leashes on the dogs and went out with a light. They led him up through the orchard, but he didn't find anyone. The next morning the police found some blood and signs of a struggle in the orchard near the high fence. They decided the injured thief climbed an apple tree and got away from the dogs, over the fence."

Matilda nodded in thought as she said, "He must have nearly evaded them altogether, to get that far. That's strange."

"Yeah, it doesn't add up. The police checked all the hospitals in the area, to see if someone came into an emergency ward with dog bites, but they found nothing. Whoever it was didn't go to a hospital. I called every doctor within twenty miles, and no one had treated a dog bite that night or the next day. Either the thief crawled off into the woods and died, or traveled a long way before he got treated."

Matilda said, "Maybe he didn't get treated at all. A little blood makes a big stain. If a tooth slashed the thief, he might have bound it tightly and avoided treatment. There's a big chance of infection from a dog bite, but it might be a chance he would take, to prevent getting caught."

"Yeah, but the idea of his getting past the dogs to the house, and getting back to the fence before they found him, doesn't make sense to me. The police bought that story, but I don't. That makes a third coincidence, straining my imagination. I've seen two unusual things happen in a case, but that's the third thing. The story doesn't hang together."

Matilda asked, "You've thought about this a lot. Tell me what you think happened?"

"Maybe it's just my suspicious mind, but there's one scenario that makes sense. I think the Calzonis came home that night and heard about an intruder chased by the dogs. According to them, they found the safe open and the jewelry gone. I think they used the intruder to explain the disappearance of the jewelry, so they could collect the insurance. I don't think the dogs chased a thief, but an intruder. I think the Calzonis waited for an opportune time to "discover" their loss."

Matilda shook her head, "The Calzonis are very substantial people. They are probably the richest family in this part of Maine. Why would they stage a theft?"

"You've asked the right questions. From what I've been told, they have more money than John Paul Getty. They don't need to cheat the insurance company, but I think they did. The more money you have, the greedier you become. It's up to us to find the answers."

"Something else, you said there were signs of a break-in. How did the thief get into the house?"

"A latch was broken on the sliding doors from the library to the patio. It's not very substantial and wouldn't have made much noise when it let go. There were marks of a screwdriver on the edge of the door. That's all it would have taken to force the lock. The Calzonis could do it as easily as a sneak thief could. There is little substantial evidence that a robbery actually occurred. The police dusted for fingerprints, but there were only those of the Calzonis. They were not smudged by someone wearing gloves, or wiped away by someone getting rid of their own fingerprints."

"The way you tell it, it seems obvious the whole story was concocted by the Calzonis, after they heard someone got caught near the fence by the dogs. Don't the police agree?"

"The police are in awe of the Calzonis. They accepted everything they said without any questions or much of an investigation. They called it a robbery by persons unknown. With that report, the insurance company had to pay."

"I didn't read about it in the Lakewood News. How did they hush that up?"

"It's not common knowledge, but the Calzonis own a controlling interest in the paper. The Beaches, who own the paper, got into some financial trouble three years ago. Their little family-owned corporation was about to go under. Richard Calzoni heard about it and offered to help. He bought sixty percent of the stock of each of the Beaches, but left them running the paper. He can tell them what to print, and what not to."

Matilda was surprised, "I didn't hear anything about that, and I know most of what happens in Lakewood. How did you find that out?"

"Accidentally. While investigating another case, I checked with the State Banking Board about insider trading. I found out about the Beaches sale then. It's not common knowledge. All the principals want to keep it confidential."

"Then there was nothing in the paper about the robbery?"

"Actually there was, but you know what I think of newspaper reporting. The Police Blotter said they investigated a reported burglary, but gave no details. A second page news article reported a possible dog-bite by the Calzoni's dogs. It said the owners were concerned, and wanted to reimburse any victim for the injuries sustained. I doubt the Calzonis got any answer to that, or if they did, they didn't let the police know about it."

Matilda glanced up from the notes she was making, "They wouldn't, would they? Let me put together what you told me. See if I have it right. The Calzonis reported valuable jewelry taken from a closed but not locked safe, allegedly while they were out of the house. That same evening their dogs attacked and injured something that climbed an apple tree and jumped over a fence, a long way from the house. The police found sliding glass doors jimmied open. They also found signs of struggle and some blood on the fence. There were no fingerprints, tracks, or anything else to corroborate their story. No one sought medical treatment for dog bites."

Hiram frowned, "That's right. I noticed you said something, not someone, left blood on the fence. Everyone assumed it was a person. What are you thinking?"

"There were no witnesses. You didn't mention any torn clothing or proof it wasn't an animal. A raccoon or even a bear cub could have climbed over the fence looking for apples. Did the police get any evidence beyond what you've told me? Did they try to get a type on the blood they found?"

"Not that they let me know about. I don't think they did any scientific investigation at all. They put out a big dragnet for the supposed thief, but stayed away from the Calzoni property after their initial investigation. It seemed they swallowed the Calzoni's story, hook, line and sinker."

"Bell Underwriters didn't. That's why they offered you the big reward for finding out what really happened to the jewels. We have some work to do."

"Right. I told you I went to the Calzoni's house, two weeks after the event. She is very gracious. He's stiff as a poker, a real tight-ass. They act as if they have nothing to hide, or are so sure of themselves that they don't mind someone poking around. I looked at the lock on the sliding doors. A stronger lock had replaced the broken lock, and the screwdriver scars were barely visible. They showed me the safe. She said how embarrassed she felt about, leaving it unlocked. I told them I'd report my findings to the insurance company, and return if there were more questions. I haven't been back. It' hard for me to admit, but I didn't like the way Richard Calzoni looked at me. For two years, I've tried to put the Sicilian mob behind me, vowing not to stir things up again. I'd like to stay in the background and let you do the investigating, especially if Richard Calzoni is around."

"Sure. I understand. It seems to me the first place to start is the fence where they found the blood. If there is fur, not cloth, on the fence, that would tend to discount the idea of an intruder. If the blood is human, it can be analyzed and typed. If it was an animal, I think they can tell the difference."

"Can they type dry blood? They always wanted a fresh sample in New Jersey."

"You remember the Shepard case, the Ohio osteopath who was convicted of killing his wife. He told the authorities he chased a man, but they didn't believe him. After he spent seven years in prison, they extracted enough materiel from the handprint on the wall to get a blood type different from his or hers. It proved there was someone else in the house that night. He was telling the truth, but they refused a new trial or a pardon. He's still in prison."

"The police hate to admit they're wrong, and judges are worse. One piece of new evidence won't get a pardon. So, you think it's possible to tell the blood type of the burglar, or even if its animal blood.

"I'm not sure. It's a new technique. If the insurance company wants to pay for an expert forensic pathologist, and if we can find traces of blood, we'll find out."

"Darn it, I've only been away from the department for a couple years, and I'm outdated. I'll have to spend more time in your library reading the journals."

"I think the delayed investigation of the Shepard case was described in Science, not a legal journal. Anyway, it's a place to start. I doubt that anyone has scrubbed away all traces of blood. Let's go see if the is any on the ground or the fence."

Hiram hesitated and then said, "I'll have to do it. You aren't licensed yet. The papers haven't come back."

"But this is an insurance investigation. As I read the law, that doesn't require a license. I can help you investigate for Bell Underwriters, can't I?"

Hiram brightened, "You sure can. I'll call the Calzonis and let them know we have to examine the fence to see if we can identify the thief. We'll look inside and outside, after we're sure the dogs are tied or muzzled."

Hiram called the Calzoni house. Virginia Calzoni took the call. She expressed pleasure that they were still trying to find the thief and recover her jewelry. She told him the dogs would be in their kennel and the butler would have the gate open and meet them at the house at two that afternoon. If they needed to talk with her, she would be home and would meet with them. Mr. Calzoni was going to be away for the day, but her man could show them the door and the fence, all there was to see, really.

Hiram said, "She was as gracious as before. She's confident we aren't going to find anything to challenge her story. She may not be the first one to trip over her own arrogance. It'll be a hard landing if we can spike her story. Richard is away for the day, so there's no chance of him recognizing me."

"Let's hope we find something useful at the fence. There's not much to go on unless we can show that there was no intruder."

"Right. Let's go in two cars. I'll go to the house while you look outside the fence. The blood was about two hundred yards east of the gate. I'll meet you there at about two-thirty. I expect the butler will be with me. I'd like to know exactly what kind of commotion he remembers."

Matilda thought for a minute before answering, "I think I'll go up an hour early and scout around the area. There may be some signs beyond the fence. I'll meet you at two-thirty."

"That's a good idea. I'll see you then."

Hiram went back to his house and Matilda got into some hiking clothes. She felt exhilarated, going to look for clues in the woods, just as Sherlock Holmes might have done.

CHAPTER THIRTEEN

Checking The Fence

Matilda parked her Buick beside the road near the entrance to the Calzoni estate. She started walking through the woods, keeping the fence in sight, but scanning the ground and trees as she walked. The maple grove was mature, with no dead branches or underbrush to impede her progress. A few scrub pine trees grew in openings in the hardwood grove. Many of the green leaves had turned red and started to fall, providing an open view in all directions. As her feet crunched through the leaves, a red squirrel chattered shrilly, disrupting the previously quiet forest. The afternoon sun filtered through the trees, making alternating shadows and bright spots. She followed a narrow path staying about fifty feet from the high chain-link fence.

She enjoyed her walk until she suddenly stopped, feeling more than seeing something in a tree ahead. She stared a large lump in the low branches of a tree about fifty feet in front of her. Then she saw two eyes fixed upon her. Finally, she realized it was a man staring at her from a perch ten feet off the ground. His brown and green jacket, hat and trousers blended into the tree trunk, but his flashing eyes and frown were enough to stop her. He glared at her and slowly lifted his finger up to his lips.

She stood still and watched as he placed an odd-looking bow and quiver of arrows on his perch, and slowly climbed down, carefully placing his feet on several pegs pounded into the tree. When he reached the ground, he walked over to her, stepping very carefully and hardly making any noise in the dry leaves. He stopped two feet from her and spoke in voice so low she could barely hear him, "What in hell are you doing here?"

Matilda started to speak but he put his hand up as if to cover her mouth. He looked angry enough to hit her. She stood still and said in a very low voice, "I'm investigating a robbery. What are you doing here?"

His countenance was black and his eyes sparking. Still speaking in a barely audible mumble, he said, "I'm hunting. Bow season opens today. You're walking on a deer trail that I've been watching since daybreak. Now you've driven anything away. Damn your eyes. Get out of here, now!"

Matilda spoke in a normal tone, "No. I'm not going anywhere. I'm meeting my partner here in a few minutes. We'll spend the rest of the afternoon tramping around this part of the woods. I suggest you find another tree to climb."

The man glanced around as her voice rose. He stepped back a step and put his hand on his hips, glared and said, "You're in the woods in hunting season. I could have shot you anytime in the last five minutes as you stomped through the leaves. Now I wish I had. At least you wouldn't have scared the deer away."

Matilda's voice raised another notch, "You be careful what you say. Threats like that will get you arrested. I have permission from the Calzonis to be here. I doubt they would have given me their permission if they knew you had pounded pegs into their tree and were perched up there waiting. I'm not trespassing, but I believe you are."

The man slumped a little, then straightened and said, "This land's not posted. I have every right to hunt here. I made that perch two weeks ago, so I could use it today. Now you've spoiled it. Damn you. Damn you."

"You can damn all you want, but don't threaten me. If you leave now, I won't report you. Otherwise, I'll have the state police here with their sirens in a few minutes. I have work to do. Just get out of my way."

The hunter turned, walked back and climbed into his tree. As Matilda approached, he brought down an odd-looking bow with springs on it, a quiver of arrows and a lunch box. He removed his hat, and spoke in a normal voice, "All right, lady. I don't want no trouble. Nothing's been through here all day. I'll go up to the Murray's orchard and stand there until sundown. What's done is done."

Matilda looked at him carefully and said, "You're Paul Bryan. I remember when you broke your arm in a ball game. Doc treats your father for high blood pressure. I'm Matilda Parker, Doc's nurse. Or at least, I was. I'm now a detective investigating a robbery. I'm sorry I spoiled your day. Maybe the Murray orchard will be more productive."

"Yeah, now I recognize you. It's OK. Sorry I was upset about being disturbed."

"No problem. Good luck."

"Thanks, but wait. Are you going to be here again tomorrow?"

"Not as far as I know. I don't think so."

"Good. I'll sneak in after daylight and try again. If I come too early, the dogs smell me and start barking. They're usually tied when the butler opens the gate at seven."

Matilda said, "If we need to come back, I'll be sure we wait until noon. I'd like to help you. You may be able to help me, if you will."

"Sure. I was upset, but I'm OK now. What can I do to help?"

"Tell me about the dogs. Do they run around the fence all night, or do they sleep?"

"I only know about the morning. I came up here at daybreak two weeks ago and they scared me out of my wits. I was walking as carefully as I could, looking for deer signs, when they suddenly started barking in my ear. I didn't realize I was that close to the fence, and they made me jump a foot. They stood and growled at me through the fence, until someone called from the house. They snarled at me, and then ran toward the house. I was real glad there was a fence there. Their teeth looked two inches long."

"Thanks. That's a help. One more thing; when you were looking for deer signs, did you see anything else interesting, any torn clothing or any blood?"

"No clothing or anything like that. There's the deer trail you were walking on, along beside the fence, and a raccoon trail leading up to the fence, about a hundred yards farther on, the way you were going. I didn't see any blood or anything like that. The leaves are falling. The maple leaves are quite red. It would be hard to identify even fresh blood without touching it. It just looked like a good place for a deer stand."

"Well, thanks. Sorry to upset your plans. Good luck tomorrow. I hope you get your deer."

"I'll be back. I'm sorry I got hot. I was stiff, tired, and discouraged. I didn't need to take it out on you."

"No harm done. Here's my card. If you see anything unusual in the woods, please let us know. There are still some unanswered questions about the robbery here several months ago."

"Gee, a robbery. I didn't know anything about that. Sure. If I see anything that doesn't belong in the woods, I'll let you know."

"Fine. Thanks. I'll keep looking. Bye."

The hunter gathered up his bow and quiver, as Matilda continued walking along the fence. On the other side of the fence, the field changed into a small orchard, with a few of the branches extended over the fence. She walked to another faint trail that she thought must be what the Bryan boy called a raccoon trail. It led to some apples on the ground under a limb hanging over the fence. As she stood there, she saw Hiram and another man coming through the orchard towards her. She waved and Hiram called out as they walked up, "Hi, Matilda. Elmer says you're about at the place where the man went over the fence. He thinks there may still be some blood on the fence or on the tree where the man climbed over. No-one has done any cleaning here, or even been here since the police looked, as far as he knows."

"Hi, Hiram. Nice to meet you, Elmer. I'm on a raccoon trail that leads directly to this spot."

Hiram looked through the fence and asked, "How do you know that's a 'coon trail? Are there tracks or something?"

"A hunter told me what it was. Paul Bryan was on a deer stand with his bow and arrow. I upset him, but he was helpful. He told me a little about the dogs, too."

Elmer frowned and asked, "What did he tell you about the dogs?"

"He said they almost scared him to death. Two weeks ago, he was scouting a place for his tree stand, and their bark startled him. He said they're usually called in about seven in the morning, so he waits until after that to come and wait for deer."

Elmer snorted, "He may get startled again. If the Calzonis are here, the dogs are let out at eleven at night, and called in at seven in the morning. When the folks are out of town, the dogs are let out whenever I want, usually about eight at night, and may not be called in until nine or ten in the morning."

Hiram said, "That's interesting. We're particularly interested in the night of the burglary. The Calzonis went out for the evening and came back about eleven. What time did the dogs go after the burglar?"

"The police asked me that, so I remember. Mr. Calzoni closed the gate when they went out, so I turned the dogs loose early, eight-thirty or nine. The rumpus started about ten. I heard the noise and called the dogs, put on their leashes, and they led me back here and barked at the tree. The ground was scuffed up and I saw a spot of blood on the tree, but no one was around that I could see with my flashlight."

Matilda asked, "Weren't you scared, alone here at night?"

"Not at all. Those dogs are better than having an armed escort. They can be vicious. Once, one of the Calzonis grandchildren started teasing one and running away. He caught her and almost took her scalp off. It was awful."

Matilda said, "I remember that, about four years ago. Doc saw her, put in some stitches and sent her to a plastic surgeon. Is she all right?"

"I guess so. I haven't seen her since. Her parents said they wouldn't visit again until the dogs were put down. Mr. Calzoni said it was the child's fault for teasing the dog. I probably shouldn't say so, but I think he likes the dogs more than he likes his grandchildren."

Matilda shook her head, and then said, "We have one other question, Elmer. What are the chances that someone could get over the fence, sneak to the house, break a lock on a window, burgle the house, and then get back to the fence before the dogs found him?"

Elmer looked at her and hesitated before he answered, "That's bothered me ever since the robbery. It had to happen that way, because the jewelry was gone from the safe. But if you want to make a bet, I'll give a hundred to one odds against someone doing it again."

Hiram said, "That's how unlikely it looked to us. We were wondering, do the dogs chase animals, if they get inside the fence?"

"I'll say. I have a small vegetable garden the other side of the orchard. The coons got in and ate all my sweet corn, just as it got ripe. They ate other things, too. The dogs caught two, but they kept coming. The coons seemed to know when the Calzonis were here, and would come early, before the dogs were let out."

"So you played a trick on them the night of the robbery. They thought the dogs would be tied until eleven. Maybe the dogs caught a coon on this side of the fence. Could that be the rumpus you heard?"

"It could have been. At first, I thought that was what happened, but when the Calzonis came home and found they'd been robbed, it certainly wasn't a raccoon that took the necklace and other things."

Matilda smiled through the fence and said, "No, it certainly wasn't a raccoon."

Hiram said, "You said there was some blood, and it hasn't been cleaned up, as far as you know. Could you show it to us now?"

"Sure, but just a minute. Matilda, there's a gate about a hundred feet further on. It's padlocked, but I can let you in."

Matilda watched as Elmer unlocked the gate. It was rusty and the grass was woven into the bottom. It obviously hadn't been opened for a long time. As they walked back, Elmer said, "In the daylight we could see the fence was covered with blood, right under that limb that hangs over the fence. There was a lot of blood on the limb and the tree, too. I don't know if any is there now. It rained several times. I'll show where I saw it."

The three examined the fence and saw some brown stains that could be rust, or could be old blood. Hiram licked a finger and rubbed a spot. He looked at his finger and said, "It doesn't look like rust. I think it's old dried blood."

Matilda said, "We shouldn't contaminate it. Let's leave it for the forensic people. I'll look up in the tree."

She quickly swung herself up onto the bottom limb, stood up on it, and looked at the branch extending over the fence, observing, "There are some of the brown stains here, too."

She leaned out onto the limb, but it bent precariously. Hiram gasped and admonished her, "Get down from there. You'll fall and get hurt. You suggested leaving the forensic exam to the pathologists. Let's do than, and not get ourselves injured."

"I was just testing. There's no way a person could climb out this limb and get over the fence. It was a raccoon or something not much bigger."

Hiram stood near the tree and said, "Let me help you get down. We've found out all we need here."

Matilda easily sat on the large limb, pushed off and landed softly on the ground beside Hiram. She smiled as if she always performed as an acrobat. His expression didn't change, but he said, "OK. We've found out everything we can here. I'd like to talk with Mrs. Calzoni. Will you come with me?"

CHAPTER FOURTEEN

Matilda Asks Elizabeth

Hiram, Matilda and Elmer walked out of the orchard, through the field, to the big house. A woman in a black dress and a small white apron met them at the door. Elmer said, "This is my wife, Ethelyn. She's the housekeeper. Is Mrs. Calzoni expecting us?"

The housekeeper smiled pleasantly and said, "Yes, dear. She is expecting the two insurance company detectives. I'll show them into the library."

Matilda passed her their card. Elmer stood back and let Hiram and Matilda walk past him. The two detectives followed Ethelyn into the library, a large room with Grecian windows facing west. A heavy woman sat in a chair by the window, reading a book. Ethelyn glanced at the card and announced, "Mr. Hiram Murphy and Mrs. Matilda Parker to see you, Mrs. Calzoni."

Mrs. Calzoni carefully closed her book, laid it aside, looked up and said, "I'm glad you could come. Please sit down. I do hope you find the necklace. It's a family heirloom that can't be replaced."

The two detectives walked across the thick white carpet, and sat on a divan opposite Mrs. Calzoni. Matilda was conscious that Mrs. Calzoni watched their feet as they walked, and wondered if they were making tracks. Hiram started, "Good afternoon, Mrs. Calzoni. Thanks for seeing us again."

"You may call me Virginia. I'm glad to help in any way I can. Do you have new information, or just more questions?"

Matilda leaned forward, "We've been looking at the place where the dogs caused something to bleed on the night of the robbery. It now looks as if it was an animal, not a person. Is there any other way a thief might have gotten away after the robbery?"

Virginia didn't reply, but stared at Matilda. Finally, she said, "We know the robber went over the fence. My husband and the police investigated. They found ample evidence that was what happened. The dogs caught him and hurt him, but he got away."

Matilda continued, "We wondered if there was any other explanation. Is there some other way for the robber to get away?"

Again, a pause and a scowl, "The facts are clear. The police didn't ask any of these questions. No. There is no other explanation beyond the obvious."

Hiram spoke more softly than his usual voice, "We understand, Mrs. Calzoni. It's our job to explore every possibility. The insurance company is paying us to find the thief and the jewelry. Can you tell us more about what was taken? Is there anything you can add to the description you gave to the insurance company and police?"

Virginia looked at Hiram and gave a faint smile, "I don't think so. I do hope you can find them. They're my most valuable possessions. The insurance money isn't important to my husband, but the jewels mean a great deal to me."

Hiram asked in his gentle voice, "Tell us about them."

"The necklace is very beautiful, diamonds and emeralds, in a Tiffany setting. The jewelry was my grandmothers.

Everything was to go to my granddaughter. They were left for me to use until she becomes eighteen. Unless you find them, her inheritance has disappeared. The poor child will get nothing."

Matilda said, "I don't understand. There must be other assets for her to inherit."

Virginia said coldly, "No, you don't understand. I am Richard's second wife. Rachel is my granddaughter, but not his. Since the accident, he has disinherited my daughter and her descendants. I have nothing left in my own name."

"Why would he do that?"

"My daughter blamed him for the injury to her daughter. She said many strong things. When he wouldn't have the dogs killed, she had a lawsuit filed against Richard. He fought the law suit and won, but didn't forgive her, and never will."

Hiram said, "We do understand how valuable they are to you. We'll do our best to find them. Thank you for your time."

"You're very welcome. I truly hope you are successful."

As soon as they got outside, Hiram said, "You catch more flies with honey that with vinegar. We need to talk about interview techniques."

"I thought she gave us a lot of information. I know she was annoyed at me, but you smoothed things over very nicely. I'm not good at beating around the bush."

"Something may jump out of that bush and bite you. Anyway, we did get some useful information. It seems the Calzonis didn't actually own the jewelry. It was being held in trust for the granddaughter."

"What will the insurance company think of that? Does that make the policy fraudulent?"

"No. It's prudent to insure anything you have in your custody. That's not unusual or illegal. The claim is valid, if the Calzonis had nothing to do with the loss."

"It seems Richard Calzoni didn't want anything to go to Virginia's granddaughter. That may be a stronger motive than the insurance claim. He sounds vindictive. Did you talk with him?"

"I tried. He's such a stiff neck; he couldn't nod if he tried. He kept saying, "I told the police everything I know. Go read their report.""

"Maybe I can talk with him. I can beat the bushes there and see what falls out."

Hiram smiled, "You've been around me too long, talking like that. I don't think you'll get very far. You could try, if he'll see you. For now, let's see if the insurance company will pay a forensic team to check for blood at the fence. That might let us know if the Calzoni story hangs together."

Hiram let Matilda out of his jeep when they reached her car. They went their separate ways, both trying to make sense of what they saw and heard.

CHAPTER FIFTEEN

Matilda Asks Doc and Zelda

At her office, Matilda made notes of everything she knew so far. There was a lot to think about. She was now convinced there never was a burglar. Maybe Richard Calzoni took the jewels when his wife wasn't looking, and blamed her for leaving the safe unlocked. He didn't need the money, but filed the insurance claim anyway. If he has the jewels, or disposed of them somewhere, he is guilty of fraud and theft by deception.

If he didn't take them, who did? Virginia Calzoni seemed very upset about their loss. She is not a likely suspect. The only other people there are the Morgans. They seem like dedicated servants, but certainly, Elmer has no love for Richard Calzoni. No, Richard seemed the most likely suspect, but how to prove that. Maybe Doc and Zelda would have some ideas. They both saw the same facts from a different perspective.

After the last patient left, Matilda and Zelda entered Doc's office and sat down. He looked from one to the other, and asked, "Is there something I need to know? Isn't the arrangement with Hiram working out?"

Matilda said, "Hiram's fine. I enjoy working with him. The problem is, I'm stuck again. I have a lot of suspicion and some evidence, but no proof. Maybe you two can make some sense of what I know."

Zelda said, "We'd like to try. Tell us about it. We'll help if we can."

Matilda looked from one to the other, then started, "You know the Calzonis, up on the ridge. Someone took jewelry out of their safe. Hiram and I are trying to find out who took it, and where it is now."

Doc scowled, "I know Richard Calzoni. He's not one of my favorite people. When his dogs chewed up his granddaughter Betsy, he was more interested in how much I was going to charge than he was in whether his granddaughter was going to live or die. If money is the root of all evil, it's growing into a tree in that man."

Matilda said, "I stayed with Betsy, preparing her for the ambulance while you talked with him in your office. I haven't met him yet, and I'm not sure I want to."

"That's another thing. I tied off the bleeders, sutured her scalp into place, and bandaged her head for transport. I called Dr. Burton, the plastic surgeon in Portland. He agreed to see her as soon as she arrived. When I called the ambulance, Calzoni yelled at me. He said his man could take her to Portland in the morning. He told me he wasn't going to pay for an ambulance. He ordered me to cancel it."

Zelda said, "My God. I wasn't here then. What did you do.?"

"He's even bigger than I am, but I got in his face, clenched my fists and told him, 'My patient will be cared for properly. Whether you pay for it or not, that girl is going to be treated right.' Perhaps my vehemence did it, but he didn't press the issue. You be careful, Matilda. I found him a hard man, used to giving orders and being obeyed."

Matilda asked, "I remember billing him several times before our bill was paid. I think we finally got something from an insurance company."

"When he found his homeowner's insurance would cover the accident, he was willing to let them pay for her emergency treatment. The girl's mother had accident insurance that helped, but I don't think that will pay for plastic surgery and long term care the girl needed. I doubt that Calzoni paid anything out of his own pocket. He's a skinflint."

Zelda said, "I don't like him already, and I've never met him. Do you have to deal with him, Matilda?"

"Probably. He's a suspect in the jewelry theft. If there was no burglar, then he is the person I'd like to hang. I think he's the prime suspect."

Doc said, "I think you'd better start at the beginning. Give us all the details and let's see if we can help."

Matilda took her notebook from her bag. Using it for reference, she related all she knew about the case. When she finished telling them, Zelda said, "I've been thinking. Unless Virginia Calzoni is lying, the jewels were in the safe when she took out her pearls at seven that evening. If she's telling the truth, the jewelry disappeared sometime after that, and before she returned the pearls to the safe, just before midnight. The dogs and fence are good evidence there was no burglar. That means one of four people took the jewels, either the Calzonis or the Morgans. You have four suspects. Can you rule any of them out?"

Matilda thought and then said, "No, not really. Some seem less likely than others, but they all had the opportunity."

Doc asked, "How about motive? Do you think Richard Calzoni took them to spite his wife and her daughter and granddaughter? He must have known the jewelry would eventually be given to the girl his dogs injured. He could be that heartless. It would mean hurting his wife and making her feel it was her fault for leaving the safe unlocked. Is that a possible motive?"

Zelda said, "He also got the insurance money. That is important to him. Rich people always seem greedy to get more."

Matilda agreed, "He's my choice for a suspect, but you're right. We have to consider all the possibilities. It's hard for me to imagine Virginia Calzoni as the thief. She seemed very distressed at the loss. She said it was the only property she had in her own name. She acted as if she had no claim on the insurance money paid to her husband. She's the big loser in this."

Zelda said, "Not really. She had them to wear, but you said she was just holding them for her granddaughter. Betsy is the biggest loser."

"You're right again. It's hard to believe even Richard Calzoni would want to hurt a child."

Doc said, "I'll believe that of him. He wasn't interested in Betsy when his dogs nearly killed her. He was more interested in his pocketbook."

Zelda shuddered and then said, "Still, you can't just ignore the other two people. They certainly had access to the unlocked safe. Can you think of any motive they might have, beyond the obvious get-rich-quick?"

Matilda shook her head, "Hiram talked with Elmer Morgan. They can retire comfortably in two more years, and they plan to do that. They both are well paid and have almost no expenses. Their food and housing, and even their car is paid for by the Calzonis. Hiram said they banked all of his salary, and half of hers, for twenty years. It's all invested in blue-chip bonds. They don't need to steal to be comfortable for the rest of their lives. Elmer might take something from Richard Calzoni, but I can't believe he'd take anything from his mistress, or her grandchild."

Zelda said, "I hate to be a spoil sport, but you also have to consider Mrs. Morgan. Does she have any motive? Does she have anything to gain by risking everything she has, at this time in her life? The jewels can't be sold very easily. The amount they will bring doesn't seem work the risk, but she still has to be considered, doesn't she?"

Matilda agreed, "All four are suspects. I guess Hiram and I will have to sort them out. You two have helped. My eyes are open wider now. Thanks."

Doc said, "I'm sure you'll get the answers. By the way, the first meeting with the staff worked out well. Zelda now has the confidence to continue. Keep in touch. We need your help as much as you need ours."

"I will. And, thanks again."

Zelda said, "Just a minute. Do either of you know what happened to the little girl after she left in the ambulance?"

Doc said, "I got a call back that night from Dr. Burton, the plastic surgeon, after he treated Betsy Lodge. He said he worked for five hours to get her face and scalp partially reconstructed. There was a lot more to be done, but she was stable in the special care unit. A week later, I got a copy of her discharge summary. It's in her chart. Dr. Burton transferred her to a plastic surgeon in New Jersey, near where her mother worked. I haven't heard anything since. The summary mentioned the name of the plastic surgeon in New Jersey. I'll contact him and ask for a follow up report on Betsy. I'd like to know how that case turned out. I'll let you know what I find out."

"Great. We can go over that when I come back next week. I may have some more definite news to report then."

Matilda left with no answers, but with a feeling that she knew the direction to take. Talking with Doc and Zelda always helped. Hiram would be at the office in the morning. There had to be some way to rule out some of the suspects. He would know the right way to proceed.

CHAPTER SIXTEEN

Matilda Asks Ethelyn

At eight the next morning Matilda met Hiram at the front door. He was neatly shaved and wore a brown cardigan sweater over a white turtleneck. She ushered him into the office where a teacart held cups and a pot covered with a tea cozy. Hiram was smiling as he sat in the green leather chair opposite the desk. Matilda poured two cups of tea, passed one to him and placed hers on her desk. Hiram took a sip and smiled again. Matilda said, "You look like a cat that swallowed a canary. You have some information. What did you find out?"

Hiram leaned back and smiled, "Finally I have one solid piece of evidence. The forensic man took several samples of blood from the fence and tree. He told me the distribution and spatters were all wrong to be from a bleeding person or animal. The answer was obvious when he first looked through the microscope. The red cells all had nuclei. It was chicken blood, not human or animal. Someone threw chicken blood into the tree and onto the fence. It fooled the sheriff, but was obviously a put up job, and not a very good one. There was no burglar. The theft and cover-up were engineered by one or more of the four people living there."

"That's great, Hiram. Now that we can prove it was an inside job, how do we find out who took the jewelry, and what they did with it?"

"First, we know someone faked a burglary, and we know how it was done. They don't know that we know that, so we may be able to trip someone up. I've talked with all four of them. You had good results in the last investigation. I'd like you to talk to each one of them, separately if you can manage it. There's many a slip between the cup and the lip. One lie leads to another. Ask them to tell you everything they can remember about that night. I'll leave the interviewing up to you from now on. Okay?"

"Sure. I'll start today. What are you going to be doing?"

"I'll be on the phone. I've started a wide search of pawnshops and some known fences. The insurance company has some people looking as far away as Boston. The necklace is much more valuable if kept together, but will probably be taken apart and sold as pieces. Even then, the emeralds are remarkable in size and cut. Finding them will let us trace our way back to the thief. I'll be on the phone to see if there is any sign of the gems."

"You talked with the four people living there. Do you have any suggestions how I should proceed?"

"Use your own judgment on that. Tell each one that you are trying to locate the jewels, and need all the help you can get. If the person is not involved, they will be eager to help. If anyone is devious or evasive, don't make any accusations, but thank them for their help. Often the guilty person tries to point you in the wrong direction. Be suspicious of anyone who starts pointing fingers."

"I'll start today. Thanks again for helping me become a detective. I couldn't have done it without you."

Hiram lifted his teacup and smiled again, "We're just getting started. I'm looking forward to a long and fruitful relationship."

Matilda smiled back and saluted with her cup, "So am I."

Hiram rose and said, "I'm going back to the cabin. I have all my notes there. Let's meet for dinner tonight. If you pick me up at the cabin about six, I'll treat you to a feast at the new Italian restaurant in North Conway."

"That sounds great. I hope to have something useful to tell you then."

"Maybe I'll have some idea where the jewelry went. Be careful today. No one seems like a killer, but sometimes desperate people do desperate things."

Matilda assured him, "I'll be careful. It's nice to know that someone cares. I'll pick you up at six."

Hiram drove away in his jeep, feeling very pleased with himself. Life was worth living again. During the long struggle getting over his injuries, he wondered if the game was worth the candle. Now he knew the effort was not wasted. He liked the way the relationship was going. There was plenty of time. The rustic character act could be turned off now. Somehow, the dread of strangers was subsiding. It was time to be himself and enjoy life. In his mirror, he saw blue smoke coming from the exhaust of his Jeep, and decided it was time to trade cars.

Matilda returned to her desk and dialed the Calzoni number. She recognized Ethelyn Morgan's voice as she answered, "The Calzoni residence."

"Good morning, Mrs. Morgan. This is Matilda Parker. I'd like to talk with you sometime today, if that is possible. We're still trying to locate the stolen jewelry and need to get all the information we can. May I meet with you sometime today?"

Ethelyn hesitated then answered, "I don't know if I can help. I have a lot to do. I don't know anything about the robbery. It will be better if you talk to Mr. Calzoni. He'll be here tomorrow. I'll arrange a time for you to meet when you call after eight tomorrow morning."

Matilda persisted, "I will talk with him, but I need to get all the facts together. I do want to talk with you. Are you free any time today?"

Another long hesitation, then Ethelyn said, "The Calzonis are in Portland for the day. I could see you about three this afternoon. My husband will be here then. He probably knows more than I do."

"Oh dear, this morning would be much better for me. Is it possible for me to meet with you about ten this morning?"

Ethelyn hesitated again, but finally said, "I suppose so. I'll be here alone. I don't think I can help you very much. I don't know anything about the robber."

Matilda said, "Thanks. I just need to get some background. I'll come at ten."

She placed the handset back on its cradle and sat looking at the phone. Ethelyn was reluctant to talk. Maybe she didn't know anything, or maybe she had something to hide. At least she could talk with her alone. Hiram felt that was important. Matilda pulled out her notebook and started making a list of questions she might ask.

Her doorbell interrupted her thoughts. She met Harry Darling at the door, gave him a quick hug and then escorted him to her office. As he sat down she asked, "What brings you here today, Harry?"

"I wondered how you were making out as a detective. I saw Hiram's jeep here earlier. How are things going?"

"Not very fast. Hiram is checking the pawnshops and fences to see if he can find any trace of the jewelry. I'm meeting with the Calzonis and their staff, trying to find out if anyone has anything to hide. Perhaps you can help."

"I'll be glad to do anything I can. What do you have in mind?"

"I'm curious about the investigation the sheriff made. The story about a thief going over the fence doesn't make sense, and we now have evidence that it didn't happen. But even before we got our evidence, the story sounded fishy. Why didn't the sheriff make a more complete investigation?"

Harry gave her a weak smile, shook his head and lowered his voice, "It's not common knowledge, and no one is supposed to know, but the reason is clear. The sheriff has to run for election every two years. The biggest single contributor to his campaign is Richard Calzoni. Not only the sheriff, but also the State Police are benefactors. When we have our annual drive for the pension fund, Calzoni always comes through big, with one condition. No one is supposed to know about his contributions. He wants it kept secret, for God knows what reason. The sheriff told me nearly half his campaign funds came from Calzoni. He wanted me to keep it confidential, and I have until now. It would be hard for the sheriff to accuse Calzoni of anything. My boss even squelched a speeding ticket for Calzoni, the only time I ever knew him to do something like that."

"That explains the lack of investigation into the robbery. Whoever staged it knew nobody would question the story. That's very convenient."

"Right. You'll have to be careful about making any accusations. Calzoni sues anyone at the drop of a hat. He usually wins, too. He has some good lawyers. You be careful."

"Now you sound like Hiram. I can take care of myself."

"I'm sure you can, but forewarned is forearmed. I had another reason for stopping in today. Have you thought any more about a ski trip over the Christmas holidays?"

"I'd like to go, but don't make any plans yet. I can't think of anything else until this case is solved. Ask me again in a month. Right now I've got to go up to the Calzonis and talk with their housekeeper."

"Okay, I'll keep in touch. I'll drop off some brochures for Aspen. They have the best package."

Harry got another brief hug as he left. He drove away, thinking, "Matilda isn't being stolen away from me by Hiram, at least not yet, but I've got to watch any competition very carefully. Matilda is so beautiful that anyone seeing her must desire her. The pharmacist she plays bridge with in tournaments has eyes for her. If only she would consent to marrying me. I know she loves me. Well, I'll keep trying."

Ethelyn wore her black dress and little white apron. She looked and acted like a proper maid. She showed Matilda into the library and sat on the edge of a chair opposite her. Because she seemed tense and apprehensive, Matilda tried to put her at ease, "It's good of you to see me on short notice. I hope you can help me. I need to know as much as I can about the night the robbery took place. Even little things could be important. I know you don't know anything about the theft, but you can give me the background I need to assess other facts."

Ethelyn remained tense and stared at Matilda briefly before answering, "I don't know anything helpful. What can I say?"

"You can help by starting at the beginning. Did you help Mrs. Calzoni get ready for the evening out?"

"Yes. I laid out her blue dress and beige pumps. She dresses herself, but I did fasten the back of her dress."

"Were you there when she opened the safe to get her pearls?"

"No. She did that while I was getting Mr. Calzoni the shoes that Elmer had polished. When I came back, she was looking in the mirror, trying to decide if the pearls or her other jewelry would be best. I told her she looked fine. She seemed unsure, but finally decided to wear the pearls."

"Did she go back to the safe then?"

"No, Mr. Calzoni said they should leave right away. She didn't go back into the library. I helped her with her wrap and they left."

"What time did they leave?"

"It was just seven thirty. I believe they were expected in North Conway at eight, and Mr. Calzoni is always punctual."

"What did you do then?"

"I tidied up the two dressing rooms and then went to the kitchen. I made everything neat there. Then I went to my room and read my book until I heard the dogs barking."

"What time was that?"

"About ten I think. Elmer let them out early, hoping to chase the raccoons from his garden."

"Was Elmer with you during the evening?"

"Most of the time. He turned the dogs loose about eight. I think he followed them for a while as they prowled around. He came up to our rooms about nine. He took a shower and was getting ready for bed when the dogs started barking. He quickly got into his clothes and called them back. When he saw some blood on Buck's nose, he put them on their leashes and went to the garden, but there was no sign of anything there. Then they led him to where they were making the fuss. That's when he found where the burglar escaped over the fence. He was gone about half an hour. When he came back with the dogs, we looked around the house. We didn't see anything, but we didn't go into the library.

So Elmer and you were together from nine until ten, but didn't see each other from eight until nine?"

"That's right."

"And he spent a half hour with the dogs before you checked the house. What did you do while he was out with the dogs?"

Ethelyn seemed to relax a little as she said, "I read my book. The dogs often make a fuss at night so I don't think much of it. Elmer hoped they were gong to catch a raccoon, and I though that must be what happened."

"When did you discover the jewelry was missing?"

"I didn't. Mrs. Calzoni did. She went to put her pearls back in the safe and found it empty. She screamed and I came down from our rooms. She was very upset."

"Did Elmer come down with you?"

"No. When he heard the car coming, he went down to put it away in the garage. He was talking with Mr. Calzoni when Mrs. Calzoni screamed. They came to the library the same time as I did."

Matilda glanced at her notebook and said, "I think I have a good idea of what happened that evening. You've been very helpful. Thanks."

Ethelyn straightened up and her eyes opened wide as she asked quickly, "What do you mean? How do you know who took the jewels?"

Matilda looked at her and waited, then said, "I meant I knew what you were doing that night. You were very helpful, letting me know where you and Elmer were during the evening. I wish I knew who took the jewelry, but I don't. Do you have any ideas?"

Ethelyn remained tense and said quietly, "Nothing you don't know. Mr. Calzoni and my husband said the burglar took them. That must be what happened. Probably if you find the burglar, you'll find the jewels. Now I have work to do."

Ethelyn stood and looked at Matilda, expecting her to leave. Matilda made another note in her notebook before closing it and standing. She smiled at Ethelyn and said, "Thanks again for talking with me. You've been very helpful in rounding out my report. May I come talk to you again if I have more questions?"

Ethelyn was very stiff as she walked to the door and opened it for Matilda before saying, "I've told you everything I know. I have work to do. Good bye."

Matilda smiled pleasantly as she asked, "You said Elmer would be here this afternoon. I may be able to re-arrange my schedule. What time do you expect him?"

Ethelyn scowled at her before answering, "He'll be back by one, but he has a lot to do this afternoon. Another day might be better."

"I only have a few questions for him. I'll stop by early this afternoon if I can. Thanks again for your help. You were very nice to see me on such short notice."

Matilda drove away feeling only partly satisfied. She had more information than before, but Ethelyn seemed to be holding something back. It might just be the reticence of a good household employee, but her anxiety was just below the surface. Ethelyn knew something that she wasn't telling. It was important to talk with Elmer before Ethelyn had time to compare notes and arrange a story, if indeed they had something to cover up. Matilda planned her next step.

CHAPTER SEVENTEEN

Matilda Asks Elmer

Matilda returned to the Calzoni Estate at one o'clock. She wanted to talk with Hiram before he and Ethelyn discussed her visit that morning. Hiram drove down the driveway behind her and continued past her car to the garage. She stood by her car as he walked back and said, "Hello Mrs. Parker. What brings you here again?"

"Hello Elmer. I talked with your wife this morning. She thought you might be able to help me with a few facts. Can we sit and talk for a few minutes?"

"I haven't had lunch yet. You could talk while I eat. I'm sure Ethelyn told you all that we know."

"I'm sure she did, but there are always details that I understand better when I hear them from different people. Thank you for seeing me."

"All right. Come in."

Together they went into the kitchen where Ethelyn had lunch ready for Elmer. She glared at Matilda but said to her husband, "Hello, Dear. I see Matilda found you. Your lunch is ready. Perhaps she will wait in the den until you've finished."

Elmer walked over, gave her a kiss on the cheek and said, "I told her she could talk to me while I eat" then turned to Matilda and asked, "Have you eaten? Would you like a cup of coffee or anything?"

Matilda smiled and said, "Thanks, but I just ate. Nothing for me. I'll just talk while you eat. I only have a couple questions."

Elmer pulled out a chair for her and said, "Please sit down. I'm starved."

Matilda sat and opened her notebook. She flipped to a partially filled page as Ethelyn put two sandwiches on Elmer's plate, poured him a cup of coffee, and stood by the sink, still glaring at Matilda. There seemed no way to get Elmer alone so she decided to proceed, "Ethelyn told me what she was doing the night of the robbery. She said you were out with the dogs before and after they chased the robber. Please tell me about that night. The more details the better. I need all the information I can get if we are to identify the thief and recover the jewelry."

Elmer took a bite of sandwich and looked at her, collecting his thoughts, then took a sip of coffee and said, "When Mr. Calzoni left, I told him I was going to let the dogs out early so they could chase the coons out of the garden. He left about seven-thirty and I let the dogs out a few minutes after he left. I watched them circling and followed them to the garden. They didn't find anything and kept on circling. I came in about eight-thirty and started to clean up when I heard them barking. I got dressed again and went out to see what they caught. I called them and put them on leashes. Buck had some blood on his muzzle. I took them back to the garden, but there was nothing there. They kept pulling me toward the orchard and took me there. They barked at the tree and the fence, but I couldn't see anything with my flashlight. I thought they chased a coon up the tree and over the fence. I saw a few spots of blood."

Elmer paused and took another bite of sandwich. Matilda looked at her notebook and wrote a couple words as she thought—this is the same story he told Hiram and me.

It's almost exactly the same, word for word, as if it was rehearsed. There must be some way to find a discrepancy.

She looked up from her notebook, glanced at Ethelyn, and asked Elmer, "You were out with the dogs for an hour after they chased the robber. It only took a few minutes to check the garden and go to the fence. What did you do then?"

Elmer swallowed and took a sip of coffee before answering, "At first I thought the dogs caught a raccoon, but then I began to wonder if it was something else, maybe even a robber. First, I walked around the house, then I checked the hen house. I wondered if something was after our chickens. The door was latched and everything there seemed all right. I looked around the house and garage, but didn't see anything suspicious. After that I turned the dogs loose again and came to our rooms to tell Ethelyn what happened."

Ethelyn spoke up, "It's exactly as I told you. Now you know everything we know."

"Yes and I thank you both. There are a few more questions. Tell me about the discovery of the theft."

Elmer said, "I was outside explaining what happened to Mr. Calzoni, when we heard Mrs. Calzoni scream. We came into the library together and found the safe open and Mrs. Calzoni hysterical. Mr. Calzoni looked at the safe and found it open and empty, then shouted at her to stop bawling and tell him how the safe got open. Finally, she told him she hadn't locked it. He was very upset at her, but finally calmed down and said the insurance company would pay for the loss. Ethelyn came down and took Mrs. Calzoni to her room. Mr. Calzoni said he would call the police in the morning. He walked around the house with me but we didn't see anything. The dogs kept circling but didn't bark again. Finally, he told me to go to bed, saying he'd lock up the house. I did as he directed."

"Then you didn't see the jimmied window in the library until the next morning?"

"No. The police found that. They came about eight and spent a half hour looking around. I showed them the fence. They saw all the blood. They told Mr. Calzoni they would report the theft, but he asked them to be discreet. He said he hoped they could catch the thief before he got far away."

"That's why the police report in the paper was so vague. Well thanks a lot. I think I have the information I need for now. If there is anything else, I'll call you. You've both been a great help to me. I can file a full and complete report after I've talked with Mr. Calzoni."

The two servants looked at each other, then Elmer said, "He's a hard man sometimes. Maybe your partner should talk with him."

Matilda smiled, "Oh, Hiram asked me to do that interview. When will he be available to meet with me?"

Ethelyn said quietly, "Please call about eight in the morning. I'll ask him. I believe he plans to be here all day tomorrow, but you will need an appointment."

Matilda closed her notebook, rose and said, "Thanks again. I'll call in the morning."

As she started toward the door, she stopped and asked, "Elmer, the next morning in the daylight, did you find anything you didn't see in the nighttime?"

"Yes, I found one of the hens was missing. There was no sign of her. I didn't see anything when I checked in the night. I thought everything was all right then, but one was missing when I fed them in the morning. It might have flown over the fence when the dogs made the fuss, but I didn't find it anywhere."

"Did you find anything else unusual in the morning?"

"No, nothing else. The police found the door forced open, and we saw all the blood on the fence, but nothing else was missing or disturbed as far as I could tell."

"Thanks. I'll call in the morning."

Matilda went back to her office and sat at her typewriter. With her notes to refresh her memory, she typed a summary of what she knew and what she needed to know. The exercise put things into focus for her. At the end of her typing, she leaned back and thought—Elmer volunteered the information about the missing chicken. If he was the one who put the blood on the fence, he wouldn't have let anyone know the chicken disappeared. He didn't know it was chicken blood. Someone else must have done it, but who? Ethelyn didn't have the opportunity and had no reason to fake a robbery. It was difficult to imagine Elizabeth Calzoni doing it. It had to be Richard Calzoni. Talking with him should be interesting.

Matilda got dressed for dinner with Hiram. She decided on her black crepe sleeveless dress and a pearl necklace. Her black pumps would make her as tall as Hiram, but she decided to wear them anyway. With her black cashmere evening jacket, she should be warm enough. There was a lot to discuss. He was finally coming out of his shell. The change in the way he dressed and talked seemed to diminish his paranoia. He wasn't as jumpy and his anxiety level decreased day by day. Maybe it was because of their friendship and association. In any case, he was good company and she was glad to give him all the help and support she could.

Just before she left to pick Hiram up, Doc called to say he had talked with the plastic surgeon in New Jersey. Doc said, "The surgery was delayed for six months because the insurance ran out and the mother had no way to pay for the reconstruction. He told me that earlier this week the mother called to ask him to schedule the surgery, saying now she could pay for it. The surgeon feels the reconstruction can be completed in three operations. He scheduled the surgery starting next week, and will keep me informed of the progress."

"That's great, Doc. I'm pleased. Maybe Calzoni finally relented and decided to do something right. I'm meeting with him tomorrow. I'll ask him."

"That could be it. Well, I thought you aught to know. Stop in and talk whenever you get a chance. Zelda and I are both interested in your progress."

"Thanks Doc. I'll talk to you soon. G'bye"

CHAPTER EIGHTEEN

Trouble In Trenton

Matilda was excited as she drove up to Hiram's cabin. Several new developments needed investigation. She was reviewing these in her mind when she saw a bright red Jeep station wagon in the driveway beside the cabin. She stopped beside it and got out to look. The paper plates and the absence of Hiram's old Jeep made it obvious he had traded cars. He came out of the house, all smiles, and shouted, "What do you think? Isn't she a beauty?"

"Hi Hiram, it certainly is. Tell me, why the new car?"

Hiram kept smiling, came out and gave her a hug. Then they stood together looking at the new car. He said, "I needed it. My game knee made using the clutch difficult, so I got an automatic transmission. The old jeep had trouble making the mountain when the snow got deep. Milton keeps me plowed out after each storm, but I was going to have to buy new tires or run chains, so I decided to splurge. The insurance company gave me a bonus for the Dr. Galliano case. They're very pleased with the work we did. Anyway, I needed a new car, and this one will go wherever I want. Do you like it?"

"It's beautiful. They'll see you coming in that bright red car. Would you like to ride with me, or go in your new toy?"

"A new broom sweeps clean. I'd like to drive, if you don't mind."

"Not at all. Are you ready to go now?"

"Come in for a minute. I'll get my coat. I have something else to show you."

They went into the cabin and Hiram passed Matilda a telegram. He said, "I didn't get any results searching for pawned jewelry in this area, so I contacted my friends in New Jersey, sent them the descriptions and asked them to check in their area. I didn't think there was much chance of finding anything, but look at the telegram."

Matilda read, "DIAMOND AND EMERALD NECKLACE PAWNED IN TRENTON FOR TEN THOUSAND STOP NOW BEING HELD AS STOLEN PROPERTY STOP ADVISE REAL OWNER STOP"

Matilda frowned at the smiling Hiram and said, "I have news too. The necklace may not be stolen. Maybe it was pawned by the rightful owner."

"What do you mean the rightful owner? Bell Underwriting paid for all the jewelry. The jewels belong to them wherever they're found. We'll get our big reward."

"There's something else to consider. Doc talked with the plastic surgeon in New Jersey about Betsy Lodge. The surgeon said the mother just scheduled the needed surgery. He agreed because she told him now she could pay for it. That means she came into some money. I wondered if Calzoni finally got religion or a guilty conscience or something and sent them money, but it's more likely the jewels found their way to them. If that's true, and Betsy is the rightful owner, then her mother pawned the necklace to pay for the surgery. It makes sense that way."

"Yeah, it makes sense, but makes things complicated. The police are going to trace the jewels back to Calzoni. I told the precinct I was investigating a robbery. They'll be upset when I tell them the jewels may not be stolen property, but that's not the worst of it. The pawnshop owner will be after the Lodges for the money. He has the right to get the money back from them if they pawned stolen property. For ten thousand dollars, he may send goons to collect it. Betsy and her mother are in real danger. If they're innocent, we've stirred up a hornet's nest."

"My God, Hiram! We've got to do something, but what? Can you find the name of the pawnshop owner? I don't know the address or telephone number of the Lodges in New Jersey. What are we going to do?"

"I can call the station and let them know the jewels may not be stolen property. They'll have to hold them, but they can tell the pawnshop owner that they are holding the necklace and may be able to recover the money for him. That might stop the bounty hunters from going after the Lodges. We can't delay. It's after six now. I'll call the station."

Hiram dialed a number and talked with someone. As Matilda listened, the conversation didn't sound very satisfactory. Hiram's voice kept rising and he repeated himself several times, then said, "Go get him."

He put his hand over the mouthpiece and looked at Matilda, "The desk clerk is a nincompoop. He's going to get the sergeant." then spoke into the phone, "Hi Mike, it's Hiram…Hymie Murphy…No, I'm tougher than a boiled owl. Listen. We have a problem. I reported some jewelry stolen. That may not be the case. Your fraud squad located the diamond necklace at a pawnshop and confiscated it. It's in your evidence locker. Can you hold the necklace and tell the pawnshop owner that we'll reclaim the necklace and pay him the full pawn ticket?"

Hiram listened and then said, "Can you find him? I know it's late, but a little girl may be hurt if he thinks he's pawned stolen property. The girl is Betsy Lodge. I don't have an address. I'm coming down. I'll explain it all when I get there tomorrow."

Again a long pause, then "OK, I'm on my way. I'll be there as soon as I can get a flight. Do what you can, and thanks."

He turned to Matilda and said, "I've got to go to Trenton to straighten this out. They may be able to find the pawnshop owner, but they may not. They'll keep the necklace locked up, but may not be able to do anything to prevent someone from harassing Betsy and her mother. Can you get an address for them? We ought to warn them."

"I'm sure their old address is in Doc's office records. They may be in the same place. I'll call now. I hope Zelda is still there."

Matilda dialed and Zelda answered. The address was in the records, as well as a home telephone number. Matilda wrote them down and passed the note to Hiram as she briefly explained to Zelda why they needed the data. She hung up the phone and Hiram said, "I know where this is. It's not in the best part of town. I'm going to call the airlines now."

Matilda said, "Wait. How long does it take to drive to Trenton? I can get to Worcester in three hours. It can't take more than another six to get to Trenton. We could drive there in nine hours. That may be quicker than flying, and we could go right to their house."

Hiram thought only briefly, before he said, "You're right. But we both don't need to go. I can take my new Jeep."

"No. I want to go. You'd be driving all night with no sleep. With two of us, one can drive and the other nap. My Buick is all warmed up and will be more comfortable. Let's go now. The sooner we leave, the sooner we'll get there."

Hiram frowned and said, "Okay, you're right. But before we go, let's try to call the Lodge house. We may be able to warn them. If they have another place to go for the night, they'll be safer. You've met them. You call."

Matilda dialed the number Zelda gave her. It rang six times before a recording said she could leave a message. She spoke to the recording, "Mrs. Lodge. This is Matilda Parker from Dr. Williams's office in Maine. You are in some danger. The necklace you pawned was reported stolen. The pawnshop or some other unsavory characters may come to get the money back. Please take Betsy and go to some safe place, a hotel or somewhere that no one knows you. Let the police know where you are, but no one else. Call the..."—and looked at Hiram who said loudly, 'The Fifth Precinct, Sergeant Harding, number 234-9876'...Matilda said, "Did you hear that?"

There was no answer from the recording, so Matilda repeated Hiram's instructions, then hung up the phone.

They looked at each other. Matilda said, "We'd better get started. I'm afraid we've caused them serious trouble."

Hiram said, "Right. I'll put a few things in a bag. See what there is in the refrigerator and the cupboard. We may not want to stop to eat."

While Hiram stuffed some clothes into a small valise, Matilda filled a bag with Ritz crackers, saltines, peanuts and a bag of M&Ms. She found a small cooler and put in a package of sliced cheese, some sliced ham and a bottle of milk from the refrigerator. She emptied an ice cube tray around these and closed the lid. Hiram emptied a coffee pot into a thermos and they carried their gourmet meal out to Matilda's car. Five minutes after the last call, they were hurrying down the mountain road as fast as Matilda dared to drive. Hiram fastened his seat belt and adjusted the pistol in his shoulder holster to make it more comfortable.

When Matilda turned right and headed for New Hampshire and Route 93 south, Hiram asked, "Don't you need anything? We may be there a couple days. We could stop long enough for you to pack a few things you might need."

"If I need anything, I can always buy it. Right now, the most important thing is getting to Trenton as fast as we can. If anything happens to those people because of us, I'll never forgive myself.

"They'll probably be okay. Now that we know their address, we could let the sergeant know and have someone watch their house. I should have done that. We'll do that at our first stop."

"I have to get gas soon. I'll stop at the next station and you can call the precinct while I have the tank filled."

They accomplished their tasks without any difficulty. With a full gas tank and the precinct notified of the Lodge's address, they relaxed a little. Matilda set the cruise control ten miles faster that the speed limit, and kept pulling her foot back from the throttle, forcing herself to resist the temptation to go faster. As the miles rolled by, they were quiet for a while, then Matilda said, "Let me summarize what I think we know. Tell me if you disagree with anything I say."

"Go ahead. We may be jumping to conclusions, but let's talk about it."

"Okay, we know the jewelry was taken by one of the four people in the house. That person faked a robbery to convince the police it was taken by a thief"

Hiram shook his head, "Maybe and maybe not."

"What do you mean 'maybe'? Do you think there was a robber?"

"No way, but it wasn't necessarily the same person who took the jewels and planted evidence of a thief. Both things were done, but maybe by different people."

"I see what you mean. Okay, then, one of the four took the jewelry. One of the four faked a robbery using chicken blood and jimmying a door."

"I'll buy that. What else do you want to sell me?"

"Whoever took the jewels sent them to the Lodges in New Jersey. We know that's where some of the jewels are now. Instead of selling some of the jewelry, Mrs. Lodge pawned the best piece for a small fraction of its real value. That means she expected to redeem it within the time limit."

Hiram nodded in agreement. "Ayah, I think we can assume part of that is a likely story. It's also possible she didn't know the value of the piece she pawned, and was pleased to get enough to pay for the surgery. Maybe she didn't plan to redeem it. It's best to stick to the facts we know and could prove, and not speculate too much."

"I'm trying to make a complete picture, but filling in the blanks with suppositions isn't helpful. I'll try to stick to facts from now on."

"Then let's back up one more step. If all the jewels went to Mrs. Lodge, and she was desperate to get money for surgery, maybe she took them all to the pawnshop. The piece found by the police was the only distinctive one. The rest may still be in the pawnshop. All we know is - the necklace was found and is now in police custody."

"Right. Can we at least assume that Mrs. Lodge pawned the necklace? It isn't likely that anyone else would have taken the jewelry to Trenton and pawned it, is it?"

"No. That's a reasonable assumption. Let's assume that's true."

"Okay, I'll start over again. Someone took the jewels from the open safe. Someone faked a robbery. Mrs. Lodge pawned the jewelry, or at least the necklace, in Trenton. The police have the necklace. They told the pawnshop it was stolen property. Is there anything else we know for sure?"

"That's about it. We'll fill in some gaps when we get to Trenton. Let's hope the Lodges got the message you left on their recorder, and believed it enough to act."

They sat in silence for a while, before Hiram said, "I had to face it sometime. It's like putting my head into the lion's mouth, but I've got to do it. I've been afraid too long. That little girl and her mother can't suffer because I'm afraid of my shadow. I'll take over the driving whenever you want. I won't be able to sleep, but I know we're doing the right thing."

Matilda kept the car rolling toward Worcester and Hiram tipped his seat back. After a few minutes, Matilda heard a rasping noise and looked at Hiram. His head was tipped back and he was sleeping with his mouth open, snoring softly. She smiled and boosted the cruise control just a little faster.

Hiram slept soundly for four hours and awoke as Matilda pulled into a service station in Connecticut to get more gasoline. He blinked himself awake and looked around, asking, "Where are we?"

"We're just outside Hartford, Connecticut. I needed to fill the tank again."

Hiram pulled he seat upright, then got out and walked around the car. He opened Matilda's door and said, "It's time for me to drive. You need to be domestic and make us a picnic lunch. My stomach thinks my throat's been cut."

Matilda got the bags from the back seat and put them on the floor between her feet on the passenger side. Hiram paid the attendant and started the car rolling again. Under the dim dome light, Matilda put ham and cheese between crackers and passed them to Hiram. She pulled out the tray in the dash and put a cup of coffee where he could reach it. She poured herself a glass of milk and they ate in silence for a while, rolling toward New York in very light traffic. The clock on the dash read one fourteen AM. Hiram said, "We'll be at the Lodges by daylight. Let's hope there's a stakeout there and they're Okay."

"I've been worrying about them. I don't know what we should have done differently, but I feel awful about causing them trouble. That poor girl has been through enough already, and now she has more surgery to suffer through."

"And what about her mother? Her daughter was nearly killed, and then she had to sue Calzoni to get him to pay for the damages. Then she lost that lawsuit. If she had any money, the lawyers would have taken it. I just hope Calzoni is guilty of something besides being a bastard. I'd like to see him hung by the thumbs."

Matilda nodded in agreement and then said, "I've been thinking. You said the money trail is worth following. He got a lot of money out of this. With the jewelry ending up in

Trenton, it's not likely that he took them from the safe, but he might have made it look like a robbery to be sure he'd get the insurance money. I know that's a theory without any facts, but it makes sense."

"We'll look into that when we get back. Right now, you should tip your seat back and try to get some sleep. We may have a long day ahead of us."

Matilda put away the rest of the food and tipped her seat back, saying, "I don't think I can sleep. There's too much to think about. I will close my eyes and relax for a while, that's almost as good as sleep."

Matilda awoke with a start when Hiram made a sudden stop at a traffic light. She tipped her seat forward and looked around. Hiram glanced over and said, "Damned city drivers. They run one stoplight then jam on their brakes at the next one. Sorry to wake you up."

Matilda looked around at the strange city and asked, "Is this Trenton? Are we here already?"

"Ayah. This is my city. I know every alley here. We're a couple blocks from the Lodge's house. The tank is empty and my bladder's full. I'm going to stop at the station on the next corner."

Hiram went to the rest room while the attendant filled their car with gas. Matilda paid him and went to the rest room as soon as Hiram came back. She washed her face and hands and looked at herself in the mirror. The sleep did little good. There were circles under her eyes and her hair was disheveled. She combed her hair and applied fresh lipstick, then went back to the car. Hiram was in the driver's seat. He looked at her and said, "Let's go to the Lodges first. I want to see if they're there and if there's a stakeout watching the place. Since I left the force, I don't know how it's being run."

They both were fully awake as he drove the last two blocks. Hiram pulled into a parking space behind a car with steamed up windows. He walked to a partially open widow and spoke to the men inside. After a few words, he came back and told Matilda, "They said they've seen no lights or activity in the Lodge apartment. They've been here since ten and are about to leave. I told him we'd go up and check. It they're all right, the stakeout can go home."

Matilda and Hiram climbed one flight of stairs and knocked on the door of apartment twelve. There was no answer. Hiram knocked more loudly, then called out, "Open up. It's the police."

When there was no response, he tried the door handle and it opened, just as a door across the hall opened behind them. A man in a t-shirt said, "Whadda ya want?"

Hiram turned and said, "We're officers looking for Mrs. Lodge. Do you know where she is?"

"I heard her leaving about eight last night. I told the officers who came about nine. They didn't look much like police officers, but then neither do you. What's going on?"

"We need to find her. Thanks. We'll just check and see if she left a note."

"The other officers had a ring of keys and opened the door. They must have found a note, if there was one. If you want me to come in too, I'll get some clothes on."

Hiram said, "No thanks. We'll take it from here. Thanks for the information."

They entered the apartment and closed the door. The place was a mess. Drawers were dumped and tossed. The upholstery was slashed. The apartment had been searched thoroughly. Hiram said, "If they found something, they wouldn't have kept tearing things apart. If Mrs. Lodge had any money here, she took it with her. Our next stop is the Precinct. I'll let the officers downstairs know there's no one here. I just hope she called and let someone know where she went."

The man behind the desk at the precinct didn't seem to know anything about the stakeout or where the Lodges might have gone. He gruffly tried to brush them off, send them away, when a man in uniform clutched Hiram by the shoulder, and said, "Well, damn. If it isn't Hymie Murphy. What are you doing here? I heard you got killed."

Hiram turned and said, "Audie. It's good to see you. They tried to kill me but I wouldn't die. Can you help us?"

"Sure, buddy, anything. Come into the squad room."

Suddenly the man behind the desk looked interested and started staring at them. Hiram frowned then took Matilda's arm as Audi stared at her. She realized she was still wearing her high heels and black dinner dress when he asked, "Is she with you, or are you bringing her in?"

Hiram smiled, "Meet Matilda, my new partner. Matilda, this is Audie Grant. We go way back."

Audie grasped the hand she held out and looked her up and down before saying, "A new partner, ay? She sure better looking than your last one. Come in, Matilda. Hymie, tell me what you're doing here, slumming?"

They went into a squad room with grey metal desks and chairs. It was deserted except for an officer pecking at a typewriter in the corner. Hiram went to a coffee urn and filled two thick mugs. He passed one to Matilda who added packets of milk and sugar. They sat down opposite Audie, who wore a big smile as he said, "Damn, it's good to see you, Hymie. Tell me what brings you to the city."

"We've come to find a woman and her little girl. They're in some danger, partly of our making. I hope she let Sergeant Harding know where she's hiding. It's important that we find her before anyone else. Can you find out if she called the sergeant, and what she told him?"

"He went home at midnight. He'll raise hell if I wake him now. I can check his desk and see if he left any notes. He may have let the desk clerk know. I'll ask him."

"Don't bother with the desk clerk. He had no idea what we were talking about, or said he didn't. We'll wait if you want to check the sergeant's desk. He used to make notes on his blotter. Maybe I can go with you."

"Sure. You stay here Matilda. We'll be right back."

Matilda finished her coffee and refilled her cup. It was strong and a little bitter, but it got her eyes wide open. Her stomach stated to growl and she wished there was something to eat. She looked at a curled up piece of pizza on a napkin on the next desk and decided against it. She started to wonder what the box on the next table held, when Hiram and Audie returned. Hiram said, "The name of the Hammond Hotel is written at the bottom of his blotter. It's cheap and not far from the apartment. It's the best lead we have. Let's go check it out."

Audie said, "I'm off until tonight. I'd like to help if I can. I've got a car."

Hiram said, "Thanks. We may need some help, but we have a car. Give me your number. We'll call if we are stuck anywhere. Right now, we'll see if we can find our quarry. You get some sleep. And thanks. I wouldn't have gotten past the desk clerk without you."

"Okay. Good luck. Plan to spend some time with me when you can. Everyone will want to know how you're doing. I'm back on duty at eight tonight, but call me at home anytime. I'm a light sleeper, mostly in naps."

Hiram drove to a run down hotel. He parked on the street and they went into the lobby. The desk clerk looked fresh and willing to help, but had just come into work and didn't know anything about who checked in the previous night. After some cajoling, he showed the registration cards to Hiram. There was no Lodge registered, but Hiram looked at each card carefully. One caught his eye. The name P. Calzoni was printed in block letters and the signature at the bottom was *P. Calzoni* in a neat script, but looked drawn rather than a natural signature. No address was given, but it did show twin beds and two occupants in room 205. He asked to use the house phone, then asked Matilda to talk to whoever answered, saying, "She knows your voice. She may be very scared. Let's hope it's them."

The phone rang twice before a small voice said, "Hello."

It sounded like a child so Matilda said, "Hello. It's Matilda from Doctor Williams's office. Is this Betsy Lodge?"

"Yes"

"Hi, Betsy. I'm downstairs in the hotel. We have some information for you and your mother. Can we come up?"

Another voice came on the phone and said, "Who is this?"

Matilda said, "Hello Mrs. Lodge. It's Matilda Parker, the nurse from Dr. Williams' office in Maine. I called and left a message on your machine last night. We're downstairs in the hotel. We need to talk with you. Can we come up?"

"No. I'm not dressed. There is a restaurant in the hotel. Betsy and I will meet you there in a few minutes."

The line clicked dead. Matilda passed the phone back to the desk clerk and asked, "Is there a restaurant in this hotel?"

He said, "Yes. They are just opening for breakfast now. Go down that corridor and turn left."

CHAPTER NINETEEN

Matilda asks Nancy

Matilda and Hiram followed directions and came to a small restaurant with another entrance opening onto the street. They sat at a booth and both ordered the blue plate special; orange juice, sausage, eggs, home fries, muffins and coffee. They were served and nearly done eating when Betsy and her mother came into the dining room.

Matilda remembered Betsy, but wouldn't have known the petite woman with her. Betsy had bangs and neatly combed hair that obscured most of her forehead, but the white scars on her cheek and one drooping eyelid were apparent from across the room. Matilda waved them over to the table and Hiram stood to greet them. Her mother acted apprehensive, but Betsy sat down and picked up the menu. They looked at each other and Matilda said, "Thanks for seeing us. I have some bad news. Your apartment was searched and turned upside down. It's a mess. Thank goodness you got my message, Mrs. Lodge."

Mrs. Lodge looked angry and said, "Call me Nancy. You'd better start at the beginning. You scared us. I heard your message when I came in. We did as you said, but I don't know why. Tell me what is going on."

Matilda said, "It's okay now, Nancy. You order some breakfast and I'll tell you everything we know. There is a lot to tell you, but no real hurry now that we know you're safe."

"Safe from what? Why are we in any danger? I'm more worried than I am hungry. What's going on?"

141

Betsy spoke up and said, "I'm hungry, Mum. Can I order while you talk?"

Her mother looked at her and said, "Sure. We can order. We'll listen while we eat. We'll find out what this is all about, no matter how long it takes."

The waitress filled the coffee cups again, took the new orders and left. Matilda took a sip of coffee and started, "I don't know how much you know already, so I'll start at the beginning. Several weeks ago, Mr. Calzoni reported a robbery at his estate. Your mother forgot to lock the safe, and the jewelry she was holding for Betsy was missing. The police investigated and found signs of forced entry and signs of a robber escaping over a fence after being mauled by the dogs."

Betsy's good eye opened wide as she said, "That's awful. Was he hurt bad?"

Matilda looked at the girl's disfigured face and reassured her, "No, Betsy. We don't think there ever was a robber. This time, no one got hurt by the dogs, except maybe a raccoon. The robbery was made up to explain the loss of the jewelry and let Richard Calzoni collect on the insurance."

Nancy said, "I didn't hear anything about that. We don't keep in touch with them after what happened. Ethelyn Morgan sends birthday and Christmas cards, but that's all we hear from Maine, and all we want to hear from the Calzonis. My mother writes occasionally, but never says anything about what's happening. She mostly tells me about her aches, pains, and medications. I didn't hear about any robbery. How are you involved, and how are we involved? We haven't been near the place for almost a year."

Matilda said, "You're involved because you got the jewelry. We're involved because we were hired by the insurance company to find the jewelry. We found out the stolen necklace was pawned in Trenton for ten thousand dollars. The police recovered it and now the pawnbroker will be coming after you for pawning stolen property. That's who trashed your apartment, and why we advised you to find a safe place."

"But it isn't stolen. It came by Federal Express with a copy of my great grandmother's will and the letters saying it belongs to Betsy. I can prove it wasn't stolen, so that's not a problem."

Hiram said, "There is a problem. You and I and whoever sent it know it wasn't stolen, but the pawnshop doesn't. They have every right to get their money back if they pawn stolen property and the police confiscate it, as they did in this case. Not only are they out the money, but they are in trouble with the law for pawning stolen property."

"But I showed the will and letters to the pawn broker. He was suspicious, but I proved that it wasn't stolen. He knows it wasn't stolen."

Hiram shook his head and said, "You think so, but when the police confiscated a necklace worth a quarter of a million dollars, he changed his mind rather quickly."

Florence opened her eyes wide, her mouth gapped twice and then she said, "What do you mean a quarter of a million dollars? The pawnbroker said it was valuable and he could give me ten thousand, but it would cost me twelve thousand to get it back. I though I might have to give him the rest of the jewelry to get enough for the surgery, but he said the necklace was enough. It can't be worth what you say."

"It is. It was appraised for the insurance policy. The other jewels are worth about as much. Do you still have them?"

"No. I left them at Burghalters Jewelry store. They told me they would do an appraisal and tell me what they were worth, and what they would give me for them. They told me they certainly were worth more than twenty thousand, but they wouldn't have an exact figure for two weeks. That's why I pawned the necklace. I wanted enough money to get the surgery scheduled, and knew I could get the necklace back by selling some of the other jewels."

Hiram said, "Then they're safe. We have a complete description of all the jewels so we'll know if they're all there. I know Burghalters, They're honest and respectable."

Matilda asked, "Who sent you the jewels, Nancy?"

"I don't know. There was no return address or letter to say who sent them."

"Do you remember the return address on the FedEx package, Nancy? They require one. That will tell us who sent it."

"It didn't though. When I couldn't find any letter inside telling me who sent it, I looked at the package. The return address was the Trust Department of the Casco Bank in Portland. It didn't make any sense then, and doesn't now. Maybe someone just used that address so FedEx would take it. That's the only thing I could think of to explain it."

Hiram said, "It makes sense to me. If the jewels were returned to the Trust Department, they would hold them. With the letters inside documenting the rightful owner, they would try to get in touch with you. The sender knew, if the package didn't get delivered to you for some reason, it would be safe with them."

Matilda mused, "Someone had this well thought out. It wasn't all spur of the moment. Probably someone waited for the safe to be left unlocked, then staged the robbery. We know it was one of four people, but there's no way to know which one."

Hiram looked at her and said, "Or which two or three. We don't want to narrow our horizons until we get more facts."

Matilda smiled at him and said, "I do that, don't I? I want to make things simple so I get ahead of myself. I'll learn if you give me time."

Nancy interrupted, "But now we have the jewels and Betsy is going to get fixed up. They do belong to her. Let's just tell everyone. What's the problem?"

Hiram said, "There are several. First, we have to get the money back to the pawnbroker. That's the only thing he understands. If he gets his money back, he'll call off his dogs. I'll talk with him. If he'll take the ten thousand and not twelve, you can give him the money and get them off your neck."

Nancy clutched her handbag and frowned, "But then I'll have nothing to pay for the surgery. Betsy is going to have the reconstruction completed. Nothing is more important than that."

Hiram said, "You don't understand. Betsy now has jewelry worth many thousands. My insurance company valued it at three hundred fifty thousand dollars. You can sell a few pieces and have all the money you need for the surgery. When you show the papers to the police, you can recover the necklace they are holding. If you let Burghalters hold that, they will easily advance you as much as you need, or you could sell them a few pieces and get twenty thousand."

"Okay, we'll do that, but I'm going to hang onto the money I have until the surgery is done. What other problems are there?"

Hiram said, "Like the woman in the shoe, your other problems are little ones. I'll go to the police station with you. I reported the necklace stolen and I can get it released when I show them you are the rightful owner. That's not a big problem. Burghalters knows me. I solved a theft for them when I worked here. They'll be cooperative and helpful. With the money to pay the pawnshop, that threat will be eliminated. You have a major mess in your apartment. You'll have to wait until the pawnbroker is satisfied before you go back there. You can afford to stay here another day or two. We should have things sorted out by then. All the other problems are for me and Matilda to handle."

Nancy hesitated, then said, "One more thing. This is a school day. Will Betsy be safe in school?"

Matilda said, "You and Hiram need to go to the police station and Burghalters, then to the pawn shop. I need to do a little shopping. I'd like to keep Betsy with me for the day, if she's willing, and it's all right with you."

Betsy looked up and said, "It's Okay. I remember you when I was hurt. I like to go shopping. School is okay, but shopping is more fun."

Nancy looked from on to the other, and said, "I'm sure she'll be safe with you. You'll be back here for dinner tonight?"

Matilda glanced at Hiram and said, "Yes, we'll stay here until you can get back into your apartment."

Hiram said, "I'll go register now. It's eight o'clock. We'll check in and freshen up. We can leave for the station at nine o'clock, if that's all right with you, Nancy."

"Yes, that's fine. I'll see you then."

Hiram registered while Matilda parked the car in the hotel garage. She went to their room and found it much larger than she expected. It was on the top floor with a view of the city. It had an ornate king sized bed and two easy chairs beside a table. She sat in an easy chair and started to doze when Hiram came out of the bathroom with a towel tucked around his waist. He smiled, picked up his trousers, took his shaving kit from his bag, and went back into the bathroom. Matilda marveled at the multiple scars on his arms and back. They hadn't discussed his injuries, but he would tell her about it when he was ready. Meanwhile she felt grubby after a night in the car. When he came out of the bathroom, she went in and showered, did her hair, applied makeup, and put on the same clothes she'd worn since leaving Maine. She returned and found Hiram dressed and smiling broadly, as he said, "They said their rooms were filled until I asked for the honeymoon suite. That's how we got this room."

They went down to meet Nancy and Betsy. Hiram hailed a cab while Matilda took Betsy to her car and asked, "Where is the best place to shop for women's clothes?"

"My mother likes Sears-Roebuck. It's in the mall."

"Okay, let's start there"

At dinner that night, there was a lot to discuss. Hiram and Nancy told how they retrieved the necklace from the precinct evidence locker, but only after two hours frustration. Burghalters agreed to hold it for her and provide an appraisal. They made an offer of $21,000 for a bracelet, which Nancy accepted. Hiram next talked with the pawnbroker. He agreed to accept the ten thousand and stop harassing Nancy, only if Hiram got a letter from the police certifying that he hadn't bought stolen property. They spent another hour at the precinct before returning with the letter and the money. The pawnbroker then told Nancy she could pawn more of her jewels anytime.

Betsy and Matilda had a successful day shopping. Matilda found Hansen's Fashions and several other stores in the mall and was now stylishly dressed and made up. The tired circles under her eyes were the only evidence of a lost night's sleep. Nancy said she'd go home and clean her apartment in the morning. By then the pawnbroker should have stopped his goons and headed them in other directions. Nancy was relieved and happy about what she learned today, and warmly expressed her gratitude to Hiram and Matilda. Last nights anxiety was rapidly forgotten as Betsy told her about the many stores that she visited with Matilda, and what they bought.

They agreed to meet for breakfast when the restaurant opened in the morning. The four rode up the elevator together. With warm goodnights when Nancy and Betsy got out on the fourth floor, Hiram and Matilda rode to the honeymoon suite on the top floor.

CHAPTER TWENTY

Matilda asks Paul

After a relaxing evening, an enjoyable night, and a big breakfast, Hiram and Matilda said goodbye to Betsy and Nancy. Hiram drove the Buick out of the city with Matilda feeling good about the way everything worked out. There were still things to discuss about the case, but they rode in silence until they crossed the George Washington Bridge, both absorbed in their own thoughts. Matilda thought about their night together, first the tired frenzy, then the relaxed lovemaking in the morning. Matilda broke the silence by asking, "You seem deep in thought. Was last night less than you expected?"

Hiram sat up straighter and looked at her. "Hey, last night was great. I'm sorry I didn't say so sooner. No, I'm worried about something else."

"What is bothering you? You've been grimacing every time I look at you. Something has you upset. If it's not about us, tell me what it is."

Hiram stared out the window for a minute before he said, "I guess we share the problem, so you need to know."

Matilda kept looking at him, still thinking about their night together, not knowing what was coming, but said, "Okay, I'm a big girl, tell me about it."

Hiram glanced in his rear view mirror again and said, "There's no one following us, as far as I can tell. I didn't tell anyone where we were staying. It's time to tell you the rest of the story. We're in real trouble."

"What kind of trouble? Tell me about it. I thought we had everything wrapped up."

"The Calzoni case is fine. It's something else. You know I was hurt bad when I came to Maine. Doc kept me alive and eventually got me well again. The department told everyone that I died. The lawyer and police commissioner arranged my transport to Maine in a hearse. That kept the goons from chasing me."

"What goons? What are you talking about?"

"Okay, I'll start at the beginning. I was undercover and worked my way up in the mob. When I got the goods on them, I blew the whistle. The feds arrested three of the dons and several street bosses. They expected to beat the rap, until I showed up and testified. After that, I was a marked man. The feds offered me witness protection, but I refused. I thought the mob was finished and I was safe, but I was wrong. They had too many cops on the payroll. I was set up and mowed down with a submachine gun. They thought they killed me, and the department went along with it."

Matilda was still thinking about their new relationship and said, "So you're dead. That's all right with me. What's the problem?"

Hiram glanced at her and said, "The problem is; now they know I'm not dead! The guys who were paid for the contract on me are still around. They're in trouble as long as I'm alive. They were paid for a half-assed job. They're in deep shit until I'm dead."

"Oh, but how do they know you're not still dead?"

"The desk sergeant recognized me. I thought he did, and I was sure when I had to identify myself to get the necklace out of the locker. He made me tell him where I worked and prove who I was. He must be one of the officers on the mobs payroll. He tried to keep me there when I went back for the letter for the pawnbroker. I had to call the commissioner to get things rolling and get out of there. I'm sure he let the mob know. They have to come after me now."

"If they're not following you, how can they find you? Did you tell the desk sergeant your address in Maine?"

Hiram glanced at her and said, "I'm not as stupid as I look. No, I didn't tell them where to find me. But they do know that I called from Maine when I reported the necklace stolen. They're not very smart, but they can make three out of one and two."

Matilda finally understood the danger he was in. His paranoia, that Doc thought was caused by his near death experience, was a real and understandable fear of men trying to kill him. The men who thought they had killed him would finish the job, or die trying. It was her problem, too. They were partners, and now more than that. Maybe learning to shoot a pistol was not as absurd as she thought. They rode in silence for a while before Matilda said, "Whatever we have to do, let's do it. Tell me how I can help."

"There's not much to do, except keep our eyes open and realize they may be coming after me. I'll be safe when I get back to my cabin. I don't know who's in charge now. The new boss may be glad I got the opposition out of the way for him. On the other hand, Junior Carrillo may be in charge, and mount a vendetta against the man who ratted on his father. I thought he was my friend, but somebody set me up. The commissioner doesn't have anyone on the inside now, so he couldn't tell me who is running things."

Matilda sat deep in thought for a while, then said, "Did you tell the desk sergeant about Nancy and Betsy? Are they in any danger?"

"I don't think so. I kept their names out of it. The pawnbroker had her name and address. The mob might get it from him. Good thinking! We should let them know. At least they should find another place to live, where no one knows them. Let's stop at the next exit and call them. They shouldn't get involved in my problems."

"Okay, let's be sure they don't suffer any more. With the money from the jewels, they can afford a better place to live. The pawnbroker's goons knew where they lived. The sooner they get out of there, the better."

At the next rest stop, Matilda found a phone and called Nancy's number. There was no answer, but the recorder asked for a message. Matilda briefly explained the situation and instructed Nancy to let the Commissioner know where they went, but not tell anyone else. Matilda said they would get her new address from him and tell them more details later. She went back to the car and asked Hiram, "Should we go back? I left a message on her machine, but she may not see the danger."

He said, "I'll call the commissioner. If he can have someone wait at the house, they'll be safe. He can help her find a place. He can do more than we could. I'll call him now."

When Hiram came back, he was grim. He said, "The commissioner said he'd have a team at the house until Nancy and Betsy got out of there. He didn't believe the desk sergeant was on the take, but he'd watch him. He'll let us know where they go, so we can keep in touch. They don't need to share in my problems."

Matilda took over the driving and Hiram slid down in the seat, deep in thought. Unless they had a lot of luck, the mob wouldn't be able to find him. He knew going back was a risk, but he couldn't let Nancy and Betty get hurt because he reported the jewelry stolen. It was worth the risk as far as he was concerned, but now he had Matilda involved and in danger. That was a real worry. Until a month ago, he felt his life was at an end, with nothing more to do except wait for the grim reaper. Now there was a future, and a responsibility. There was nothing more to do now except watch and wait.

Matilda interrupted his thought and asked, "With the jewelry found and in the hands of the rightful owner, where does that leave the insurance company?"

Hiram roused from his reverie and said, "I've been thinking about that. The jewels weren't really stolen, but they were taken from Calzoni's safe while they were in his custody. Unless he tried to fake the robbery, his claim may be legitimate. If so, we may not get us our bonus. If Richard Calzoni faked the theft to get the insurance money, that's fraud, and they can get their money back. We're still working for the insurance company. There is more investigation to do. Somebody jimmied the French window in the library. Someone put chicken blood on the fence and tree. If we get can figure out who that someone is, we may get the answers the insurance company needs."

Matilda said, "I've been thinking, too. I haven't met or talked with Richard Calzoni. With what we now know, isn't that the next logical thing to do?"

"You're right."

They stopped for lunch and filled up with gas in Connecticut, and arrived in Lakewood at five that evening.

Matilda dropped Hiram off at his cabin and refused his offer to make them supper. She wanted to go home and check for messages, and looked forward to a night in her own bed. He said he'd come to the office in the morning.

Matilda found her answering machine held several messages. Zelda invited her to play bridge on Wednesday. The other messages were unimportant until she heard a familiar voice say, "Mrs. Parker. This is Paul - Paul Bryan. We met in the woods by the Calzonis. I was hunting. You said I should let you know if I found anything in the woods. I found something. My number is 647-0102."

Matilda glanced at the clock—not quite six. She dialed the number and Paul answered. She said, "Hello, Paul. This is Matilda Parker. I got your message. Thanks for calling. I'm very interested in what you found. Tell me about it."

"Sure. When I went back to my stand, I walked along the fence looking for deer signs. I found some coveralls and a pair of boots in a pile beside the fence. It looked like someone threw them away. The boots were no good to me, but the coveralls were big enough so I took them and put them in my trunk. I thought they might be handy if I had a flat tire. Then I thought about what you said and called."

"I'm glad you did. It could be important, or could be nothing. When can I see the things?"

"I can go get the boots in the morning if you want. They're still in the woods. If you just want to see the coveralls, they're in my trunk and you can see them anytime."

"I'd like to see both, and I'd like to go with you to get the boots. Can we meet at the grove in the morning? You can show me where you found the things."

"Sure, if you don't mind a hike. I can be there at seven. The dogs should be gone by then."

"Great. I'll meet you at the grove at seven. And thanks again."

"No problem, bye."

Matilda was excited. Maybe Paul's discovery had some bearing on the case, or maybe someone just discarded some old clothes. In either case, there was real detective work ahead of her. She made one more call to Hiram and told him the news. She said she'd call him after she met with Paul. After a light dinner, she went to bed and tried to concentrate on the book about firearm safety, but laid it aside and fell asleep.

Paul was waiting when she got to the grove in the morning. The sun was bright and the fall air crisp and clear. Paul opened his trunk and lifted out a large denim garment. He held it up and said, "It's big enough to cover anything I might be wearing. It's stained, but would keep me from getting my clothes soiled."

Matilda looked at the coveralls he was holding. There were numerous dark brown stains over the front. Otherwise, they looked clean. She said, "Those could be blood stains, Paul. Have you worn them since you got them?"

"Naw. I just threw them in the trunk. I haven't killed anything or put anything in the trunk to get on them. They were like that when I found them."

Matilda got a large plastic bag from her car and had Paul put lower the coveralls into the bag as she held it. She filled out a label and had Paul sign it, then tied it to the bag, and locked it in her trunk. With two more big plastic bags in her pocket, they started into the grove. Paul walked at brisk pace and Matilda was glad to get the exercise. In ten minutes, Paul stopped and pointed to a pair of boots lying on the ground. He said, "The coveralls were wrapped around them. They fell out when I picked it up. They're much too big for me. I just left them."

Matilda said, "Let's put them in a bag, too. Let's not touch them. Put a stick inside and lift them that way. I may want to check for fingerprints."

Paul looked at her and asked, "Then this may be evidence? I did the right thing to call you?"

"It could be important. I don't know. But let's handle it as if it was evidence."

They put the boots into a bag without touching them, tied the top and attached a label. Matilda looked around and asked, "Were these white feathers here before, when you found the stuff?"

"Yeah. There were a couple on the coveralls, but I shook them off."

Matilda opened the last bag and said, "Let's put what we can find in this bag. I think I know where they came from."

Paul said, "This is great. Are the feathers a clue? I've never helped an investigator before. Can you tell me what it's all about? You said something about a robbery when I was hunting. Do you think the robber used these boots?"

"I'll tell you all about it when I get the answers. Yes, the clothes and feathers are clues. Right now, I have to get these analyzed. I really appreciate your help, but I can't tell you anything more until I get some answers."

"I understand about jeopardizing an investigation. I won't say anything until I hear from you, but I am curious."

They chatted as the walked back to the car, Paul carrying both plastic bags. Matilda decided that Paul was intelligent and discrete, and might be useful in future investigations.

She drove to Hiram's cabin with the three bags in her trunk, feeling good about herself, a real detective.

Hiram was pleased to see her and gave her a hug as she said eagerly, "I have the clues we need. I think we can find out who put the chicken blood on the fence."

Hiram stepped back and said, "The tea is hot. Let's have a cup while we talk."

As they sipped their tea, Matilda told him about bagging the boots and coveralls, and the few feathers they found near the fence. She said, "The stains look like blood to me. Can we get them examined?"

"Sure. The forensic lab the insurance company uses can do it. They identified the chicken blood. I'll have to take the bags to Portland. What's next on your agenda?"

"I want to meet Richards Calzoni. I think he has the answers we need."

"He's a hard man, stiff as a poker. If you get anything out of him, it'll be like getting blood out of a turnip. What approach will you use?"

"I'm not sure. How much should I tell him? He doesn't know Betsy has the jewels. I may get more information without telling him. On the other hand, he might open up if he feels he could lose the insurance money."

"You'll have to play that by ear. I've found the more facts I have that the suspect doesn't know about, the easier it is to find things out. One lie leads to another until the suspect trips over them."

"Okay. I'll just ask some questions. When will we know about the things you're taking to Portland?"

"They work fast. They should be able to tell if the stains are blood in a couple minutes. Dissolving them and looking under a microscope takes only another few minutes. Typing takes longer, but if it's chicken blood, they don't need to do that. I expect to have some answers when I come back tonight."

"How about finger prints, or some other way to identify the boots? Can they do that?"

"Sure, they can dust for prints and lift any good ones, but they can only identify them if they have something to compare them with. Unless they have something to go on, they have to send the prints to the FBI, and that takes quite a while to get an answer. Unless Calzoni was in the service or had some other reason to have his prints on file, they may not be able to tell us anything."

"Then we need something with fingerprints on it. That's a challenge for me."

"You be careful. This isn't a murder investigation, but some people are more concerned about money than they are about lives. Calzoni strikes me that way."

"I'll be careful. I'll put the bags into your Jeep and go see if Calzoni is home. I won't call ahead this time. Wish me luck."

Matilda drove down the Picked Mountain Road wondering what she should say to Calzoni. Then her thoughts changed to forensics, deciding to get a book and read about evidence gathering. The simple office test for blood in the stool using guaiac should work on fabrics. Lifting fingerprints seemed simple enough. Then she thought about getting a sample of Richard Calzoni's prints. She changed directions and went to her house. She found a big tan plastic purse with smooth sides and no handles, washed it with soap and water, rinsed it thoroughly and wiped it with a soft cloth, being very careful not to touch it with her hands. She changed into a beige suit and put on beige gloves to match. Feeling prepared and clever, she drove to the Calzoni estate.

CHAPTER TWENTY-ONE

Matilda asks Richard

Matilda drove to the house and parked her car. The dogs came and smelled her but didn't bare their teeth. She ignored them, walked to the front door and rang the bell. Ethelyn answered the door, asked her to stop into the foyer and said she would announce her. She came back and said, "Mr. Calzoni will see you. Follow me, please."

A very large man rose to greet her when she entered the library. He was well over six feet tall and very heavy, nearly three hundred pounds by her nurses estimate. He said, "My wife said you were here. Have you found the thief?"

"Hello, Mr. Calzoni. We have some good leads, but haven't apprehended anyone yet. The insurance company wants us to continue our investigation. We appreciate your cooperation."

He sat down and looked at his wife before answering, then said, "We told the police everything. They did the investigation. What do you want from us?"

Matilda took the notebook and a pen from her purse and said, "Thank you for your help. We are trying to get the exact modus operandi of the thief. The more we find about exactly how the robbery occurred, the more we can narrow down the suspects. We talked with the others, but would like to have you describe what you saw and did that night."

Richard harrumphed and scowled at her, then said, "All right. We came home about eleven. I was outside, talking with Elmer about the intruder the dogs chased away, when I heard my wife scream. We ran into the house and found her in the library, hysterical. She left that safe unlocked and her jewelry was gone. I went with Elmer to the fence and saw where the thief escaped. There was nothing more to do that night so we went to bed. I called the police in the morning. They made a full report. What else can I tell you?"

"Tell me about the weather. Was it raining? Did you need to change clothes before you went to the fence?"

"The weather was clear. The moon was bright enough that we hardly needed the flashlight. I didn't stop to change my clothes. For goodness sake, what kind of a question is that?"

"It's important. One thief we know only works on dark rainy nights. Another thing, when did you find the door pried open."

"The police found that in the morning. It's in their report."

"Then you did no more investigating that night, after looking at the fence?"

"There was no need. The thief was gone. The dogs were loose again. We went to bed."

As her husband said this, Matilda saw Elizabeth Calzoni stiffen, then catch herself and settle back into her chair. Matilda entered a note in her notebook before saying, "I think I have a clear picture of what happened now. I'll put this together and make my report. May I call again if I have any more questions?"

"Damned if I know what more help we can give you. You've bothered us enough. Elizabeth feels badly enough about this without you stirring things up. Just leave us alone."

"Right. I'll only come back if it's important. Thank you for your cooperation. The insurance company appreciates it."

Richard arose and Matilda took off her glove to shake his hand. He held his hand out reluctantly, then moaned as Matilda dropped her purse. He stooped and picked it up and passed it to her, saying gruffly, "Good bye. I don't expect to see you again."

Matilda held her purse in her gloved hand and walked to the door with Ethelyn, who held the door open and acted as if she wanted to say something. Matilda stopped just outside the door and waited, but Ethelyn just sighed, turned and went back into the house. Matilda carefully opened the car door with her ungloved hand and placed the purse on the seat. Before starting the car, she picked up the purse with her gloved hand, put it into an evidence bag and tagged it. She saw Elmer watching her from the garage door, waved and drove away, heading for Hiram's again. If she got there before he left for Portland, he could take the purse for fingerprint comparison. She met him on a corner at the bottom of the narrow Picked Mountain Road. They skidded to a stop, bumper to bumper. He got out, walked up and said, "I'm glad this isn't my old jeep or I'd be in your back seat. As it is, my brake foot is slow. What's your rush?"

Matilda took a deep breath and effused rapidly, "Sorry, Hiram. I wanted to catch you. I have Richard Calzoni's fingerprints on this purse. They will be the only prints on it. If they match the boots, we know he's lying and faked the robbery, or at least put the blood on the fence. Then the insurance company will get their money back and we'll get our bonus."

"That's almost enough reason to get me killed, but not quite. Okay. I'll take that bag with the others. With any luck, we'll have evidence enough to have the company ask Calzoni to return the money. Did you find out anything else?"

"Not really, but Elizabeth Calzoni acted as if he was lying when he said they went to bed without any more investigation. I need to talk with her again. Also, it seemed as if Ethelyn had something more to say, but I didn't have the opportunity to talk with her again. I'll keep working while you're on Portland. Give me a call when you get back."

"I will. Maybe we can have dinner and celebrate."

. Matilda backed up to a wide place in the road to let Hiram get past and head for Portland with the evidence bags. On the way to her house, she planned her next step. It seemed the large coveralls and boots belonged to Richard. If forensics proved he was the one who killed the chicken and put blood on the fence, that was good for the insurance company, but it didn't explain who sent the jewelry to Betsy. Both Elizabeth and Ethelyn had something to tell. How to talk with them was the next problem to solve.

Matilda thought for a long time, then called the Calzoni house. Ethelyn answered, "The Calzoni residence."

Matilda said, "Hello Ethelyn. This is Matilda. I would like to talk with you alone sometime. I have some information about Nancy and Betsy."

There was a long pause, then Ethelyn said, "Thank you for calling. I do need my prescription filled again. I will come to see the doctor this afternoon. I'll try to be there at the start of his office hours."

Matilda hesitated only a moment and said, "We'll see you then. Goodbye."

Matilda hung up the phone, marveling at Ethelyn's quick thinking, but then remembered that she wanted to say something when Matilda was leaving the house. The call from Matilda was not as big a surprise as it might have been. This piece of the puzzle was going to fall into place. The next step was talking with Virginia Calzoni. That was not going to be easy as long as her husband was around. She seemed quite dominated by him. Maybe Ethelyn could help her with that when she saw her at noon.

Matilda called Zelda. There was no problem using an office for an interview. Zelda would usher Ethelyn back as soon as she arrived. Zelda suggested that Matilda come early and share a pizza with her in the break room. They agreed to meet at noon so Matilda could tell all about her progress in solving the case while they ate. With that resolved, Matilda turned to her typewriter to put her notes into better order. Hiram appreciated her detailed reports, and this time the insurance company would need enough documentation to go to court, if necessary.

Lunch with Zelda was pleasant. Doc stopped by to say hello and ask her to come back after office hours whenever she could. He wanted to tell her about a couple medical examiner cases and get her opinion about his decisions. She told him that Betsy was going to have the surgical reconstruction completed. He left with a big smile on his face.

Zelda said the office staff was cooperating with her. The scheduled office meetings had worked. Even the negative employee was grumbling less. Being office manager was now enjoyable for Zelda. She was studying books on management and business administration, thinking this might be something she might pursue in college.

Matilda told of her trip to New Jersey and what they found there. Zelda was interested in hearing more about Hiram and the personal relationship, but Matilda just told her they enjoyed working together and had a pleasant trip.

At one o'clock Zelda ushered Ethelyn into a small examining room where Matilda was waiting. Matilda greeted her warmly but Ethelyn was wary and sat stiffly in the chair as Matilda sat on a stool facing her. Ethelyn said, "What about Betsy. Is she all right?"

"She's fine. We went shopping together. She's a delightful young lady."

"She certainly is. I'm very fond of her. I don't have any children and Betsy is very dear to me. She calls me Aunt Ethelyn, even though it upsets her grandfather. You said you have some news. What is it?"

"She's finally going to have the surgical reconstruction of her face and scalp. Her mother now has the money to pay for it. Do you know how she got the money?"

Ethelyn sat and stared for a minute before saying, "Yes, I do. When Mr. Calzoni wouldn't give her the insurance money, I sent Nancy the jewels."

"Tell me about it. Did you think the insurance money would go to Betsy or her mother? Is that why you took the jewelry?"

"I did think so. Mrs. Calzoni felt very badly that Mr. Calzoni wouldn't pay for the surgery. Once she told me he wouldn't let her send them the jewels, or even write them a letter. I sent Betsy birthday and Christmas cards with little notes. Nancy wrote me twice, in plain envelopes with no return address, to let me know she was trying to save money for the surgery. I knew about the insurance policy, so I thought if I hid them, Betsy would get the money for the surgery."

"So you took the jewels from the safe and hid them. What happened then?"

"The police came and looked, but Mr. Calzoni convinced them a robber took them and escaped over the fence. They looked at the safe and the fence, and found the marks where someone pried open the glass doors. They left and didn't come back."

"Did you pry open the door to make it look like a robbery?"

"No. I just took the jewels and hid them. I don't know when the marks were made on that door. I didn't do it. I was as surprised as anyone."

"Do you know anything about someone taking a chicken from the coop, or going back to the fence that night?"

"No. The next morning Elmer told me a chicken was missing. Why is that important? The chicken might have run away, or got caught by a fox."

"Think about it Ethelyn. With the dogs out, could a fox get into the chicken coop? It may not be important, but it did happen the same night you took the jewels."

"But I still don't see what that has to do with anything. Maybe Elmer counted wrong and it wasn't there the day before. I don't know."

"Did Elmer stay with you after the Calzonis came home?"

"He went to the fence with Mr. Calzoni. They looked around the grounds for a while, then he came to bed."

"Did he leave again that night?"

"No. He's always up early in the morning and likes to go to bed as soon as he can. It was very late, after midnight, when he came in. He went right to bed. He gets up at five every morning and needs his sleep."

"I'm sure he does. Did he bring you here today. Is he outside?"

"He said he'd be back in a half hour. He's probably in the waiting room."

"Do you mind if I have Zelda bring him in here? Does he know that you took the jewels?"

"I didn't tell anyone, but I don't care if he knows. I intended to tell him, but he's been upset, thinking Mr. Calzoni might blame us for letting the jewels get stolen. I don't think I did anything wrong. The jewels were rightly Betsy's and she needed them. I thought she would get the money and I could give the jewels back. Then Mr. Calzoni got the money for the jewels and kept it. I'd like Elmer to know what I did. It may be easier if you are here. Yes. Ask him to come in."

Zelda found Elmer in the waiting room and brought him back to the examining room. She brought in another stool, but Elmer stood beside his wife, looked at Matilda and asked, "What's the matter? Is her blood pressure high again?"

Matilda reassured him, "She's fine. We've been talking about the missing jewels. She wants to tell you something."

Elmer looked at his wife and sat on the stool. He just looked at her as she said, "Elmer, I took the jewels. I hid them so Betsy would get the money for the surgery."

Elmer stood quickly and shouted, "You did what? Mr. Calzoni will have you in jail. You know how mean he is.

Why would you do a thing like that? We've got to give them back."

Ethelyn remained calm and said, "Don't shout. I took them so Betsy would get the insurance money and get her face fixed up."

In a lower voice, but still upset, Elmer said harshly, "We've got too put them back. Where did you hide them?"

"I sent them to her. When he kept the insurance money, I sent them to Nancy so Betsy could get her surgery."

"Well darn, what are we going to do? I made it look like a burglary so we wouldn't be accused. Now I'm as guilty as you are. What are we going to do?"

Matilda interrupted and asked, "Elmer, what did you do to make it look like a robbery? Did you take the chicken?"

Elmer looked at her, then back at Ethelyn, before answering, "What's the missing chicken got to do with anything? We may be going to jail and you're worried about one chicken!"

Matilda answered, "Maybe nothing, but how did you make it look like a robbery?"

"I forced the lock on the French door. I was afraid Mr. Calzoni would accuse us of not locking the house, so I pried the door open when I got up in the morning. Now I'm as guilty as she is. What are we going to do?"

Matilda spoke softly but with a reassuring voice, "Let's leave the rest up to me, Hiram and the insurance company. Don't tell anyone else what you told me. You haven't done anything illegal, maybe a little vandalism but that's not a big deal. No one needs to know about that. I'll tell you something to reassure you. Someone took the chicken, cut off its head and spread the blood on the tree and the fence to make it look like a robbery. It had to be your boss. He faked the robbery so he could collect on the insurance policy. That's a crime. He'll have to give the money back, and may face criminal charges. The jewels went to the rightful owner, so there was no theft. For now, don't tell anyone what you did or what I told you. Can you do that?"

Elmer put his arm around Ethelyn and she took his hand. They looked at each other and Elmer said, "Sure. We won't tell anyone. I'm glad Betsy is going to get fixed up. We won't say anything, if you say that's okay."

Ethelyn said, "We've been talking about retiring. We could do it now and not wait. I'd like to get away from that awful man."

Elmer said, "Let's talk about that on the way home. We can retire now as well as later. There's no reason for you to put up with that bear any longer."

Matilda thanked them for coming and showed them out. She waved to Zelda and went back to her office to type her progress notes and wait for Hiram. She just put the last sheet in her file when Hiram arrived, all smiles. After a brief hug, he said, "They were impressed. Chicken blood was spattered all over the coveralls and boots. The only fingerprints on the boots matched the prints on your purse. We can't prove he jimmied the door, but even without that, there is solid evidence that Calzoni staged the robbery. He knew no one would believe that a thief made it past the dogs to the house and back, without some convincing clues. We have enough evidence to force him to reimburse the insurance money. The company may want to sue him for fraud, but that would just make the lawyers rich. We'll get our bonus."

Matilda said, "That's great. Actually, I found out he didn't force the library door, but we don't need to tell anyone that. With proof that he spread the chicken blood, the forced door will obviously look like a part of his deception."

They sat looking at each other, feeling very satisfied, when Matilda said, "I'm not eager to confront him with what we know. Maybe we should go together."

Hiram said, "We don't need to do anything more except give a complete written report to the insurance company. They will do whatever needs to be done. Our job is finished with the report. Probably you should start putting that together."

Matilda passed him a thick folder and said, "Read through this. If you think anything should be left out, strike a line through it. If something should be added, just tell me. It's rough now but I can type the final report in an hour. While you read and edit, I'll type the last pages from what you just told me. We can attach the forensic report and send it in."

Hiram glanced at the thick report and started reading before he looked up and said, "We make a great team. Let's think about making a more permanent relationship."

Matilda looked up from her typewriter and said, "I like the way things are working out. I think Murphy Investigations is here to stay."

He smiled at her, thought about saying more, then returned to reading the report. There was no hurry. Everything was turning up roses.

CHAPTER TWENTY-TWO

Trouble in Lakewood

Matilda smiled at Hiram when the office phone rang. She picked it up on the second ring and said cheerfully, "Murphy Investigations, Matilda speaking."

A gruff voice asked, "Is Hiram Murphy there?"

"Yes, just a minute." Matilda held the phone out to Hiram with a quizzical look as she said, "It's for you."

Hiram put down the report and took the phone, "Hello, this is Hiram."

Matilda watched as Hiram listened for a long time, a frown growing on his face. He said, "Thanks, Commish. They'll need all the help you can give them. The Lodges are good people who are caught in my mess. Please keep us posted. If we can do anything, let us know."

He listened again and said, "Yeah. I thought the desk clerk recognized me. I'll be ready for them. Thanks."

Matilda looked at Hiram's narrowed eyes as he passed the handset to her. He looked more worried than she had ever seen him. He said, "They know."

"Who knows? Tell me."

"The mob. They got Nancy's address from the pawnbroker. The deskman must have told them. When she came to pick up Betsy at school, she wasn't waiting for her. Nancy rushed home, saw the police car outside and ran into her apartment. The phone was ringing when she go there. A voice told her Betsy would be fine if she told them what they wanted to know. She told them everything she knew, your name and mine and where we live in Maine. They told

171

her Betsy was walking home. She ran downstairs and saw Betsy walking toward her. She ran to her and the police followed. The police stayed with them while she packed their clothes, then they went down to the station in the police car. The commissioner talked with them and found them a safe house. He said Nancy doesn't plan to go back to her apartment again. The furniture was all smashed and she plans to start new somewhere else. They're probably safe now, but we aren't"

"Do you think the mob will send someone to Maine?"

"They're on their way. Not one, but several. They were paid for killing me. Either they finish the job, or they'll be killed themselves. It a matter of honor for them. At least the commissioner was able to warn us. We can get ready."

Matilda stood up, then walked briskly toward the door as she asked, "Do we have to stay and wait for them? We can go to Canada or somewhere. I'll go pack."

Hiram sat still and shook his head, "Running isn't the answer. The Sicilian mob covers the globe. There's no place to hide. If this bunch is killed trying, they may not send anyone else. When the people paid for doing a job get themselves killed, the slate is clean. I know how they work. I lived with them for three years."

Matilda walked back and asked, "What do we do? How can we stop them? I can't use a gun, unless you show me how right now."

"We have to have a plan. Is your State Police Sergeant friend reliable? We could use some help from someone we can trust."

"Harry is as reliable as they come. He'd do anything for me. He likes to take charge, but if you handle him right, he may do what you want. Should I call him now?"

"Yeah. Give him a call. I'd like to talk with him. Together we can make a plan."

Matilda called Harry's house but there was no answer. She called the barracks and was told they'd radio him to call her. In ten minutes, he was on the phone, "Hi Matilda. What's so urgent? I'll be home tonight."

"We have a big problem Harry. We need your help here in Lakewood. Can you come and talk with us?"

"Sure, I'm on patrol in Lakeport, but I'll come right now. What's this about?"

"We'll tell you when you get here. Come to my place. Thanks."

Harry parked his cruiser in the driveway and rang the office bell. Matilda opened the door and gave him a more vigorous hug than usual. She said, "Thanks for coming so soon. Come in and meet Hiram."

Harry and Hiram shook hands and sat in the leather chairs facing each other as Matilda sat behind the desk. Harry looked from one to the other and asked, "What's this about?"

Matilda started, "Oh, Harry. We're in big trouble. There are some gangsters coming from New Jersey to kill us. We need your help."

Harry sat back, shook his head and looked first at one, then the other before saying, "Hang on a minute. You're way ahead of me. This is Maine. Why would gangsters be coming here? And why are they after you? You better calm down and start at the beginning. Nothing makes any sense yet."

Hiram said, "Maybe I can explain. It's me they're after, not Matilda. I was an undercover officer in New Jersey. I lived with the mob for three years, finally getting enough to

173

put the big guys away. When I testified at the trial, they put a contract on me. One of the officers in my precinct set me up and I was riddled with a tommy gun. They thought I was dead, and the force let them think that. They almost killed me, but when I got out of intensive care, an ambulance brought me to Maine and Doc patched me up. This week we had to go back to New Jersey to keep a little girl from getting hurt, and they recognized me. My commissioner told me they're coming for me now. That's why we called you."

Harry frowned and said, "Okay. Then Matilda isn't involved. That's a relief."

Hiram said, "No. It's my problem. She doesn't need to do anything."

Matilda started to protest but Harry looked at her and said, "As long as she's not in any danger, I'll help you any way I can. I can't do anything until they commit a crime. There's no law against coming to Maine. If I wait until they start shooting, it's too late for you, Hiram. What do you have in mind?"

"My cabin is on Picked Mountain with only one road to get there. The goons are city people and won't try to climb up over the cliffs. I felt safe there while I was getting my legs under me. I can hear a car climbing the hill from a half mile away. I have a rifle and can defend myself pretty well. The log walls will stop a bullet, but if I get them pinned down, they can wait it out and come in after dark, or even burn the place down."

"Then you want me to come after the shooting starts. I can block the road so they can't get away, but I can't just wait around. I have other things to do. When do you think they will come?"

174

"They're on their way now. I know how they work. Junior Carrillo will have a bug up their ass. He likes Lincoln Continentals and has several, all black. They keep an arsenal in the trunk. The commissioner said he sent two or three goons as soon as they got the information from Nancy. They were probably on the road by six o'clock. It's a nine-hour drive. They'll take turns driving. They'll be in Lakewood before daylight."

Harry thought a minute and said, "If I know it's a black Lincoln Continental with New Jersey plates, I can watch the road and stop them."

Hiram said quickly, "That's dangerous. Two highway patrolmen were shot when they stopped a Carrillo car in New Jersey. These men have their lives on the line. Unless you have ample backup, you could be killed."

"Okay, thanks, I'll just watch for them and call you if I see them. I can alert the other State Troupers to keep their eyes out for the car and let me know if they see it. The Maine Turnpike tollbooth operators have helped us before. They call the barracks if they see someone suspicious or obviously drunk. I'll let them know a black Lincoln with New Jersey plates and two or three men should be coming through about two in the morning. They'll let us know if you're right about them coming."

Hiram said, "That will help, but something else has me worried. We didn't tell Betsy or Nancy where I live, so they don't know about the cabin. They can ask people where I live after they get here, but very few people in Lakewood know me. The sign out front of here is all most people know about me. They'll probably come here first."

Harry looked at Matilda and said, "We've got to get you out of here. Put some things together and I'll take you to my place."

Matilda sat still and said, "I'm not going anywhere. They may find out Hiram lives on Picked Mountain and go directly there. If they come here, they'll want to know where Hiram lives, and I can tell them. Then, I can let both of you know they're on their way. You'll have ample warning and can trap them. They have no reason to hurt me. I'll be okay."

Both Hiram and Harry protested, but Matilda was adamant. She wanted to help and didn't see any danger in her plan. Harry and Hiram both had strong reservations, but finally decided she would be safe if Harry stayed within sight of Matilda's house, while Hiram got his cabin ready for the assault. If they came here first, Harry would follow the Lincoln when they headed for the mountain. If Hiram heard a car coming up his road, he would call Matilda and she could let Harry know. After both men admonished Matilda, warning her not to do anything stupid, they left and she went to bed, with her alarm set for three o'clock.

All three tried to get some rest, without much success. Hiram spent an hour checking and reloading all his rifles and shotguns. He could fire his rifle through his slits without any chance of being hit. He filled several pails and pans with water in case they tried to start a fire. He put boxes of ammunition in strategic places and strapped on his shoulder holster, He lay down on his cot, but didn't feel at all sleepy, worrying that Matilda might try something foolish. He regretted leaving her alone. Even with Harry watching the house, the goons could hurt her just for spite.

They were desperate, and capable of anything. It was a long night.

Matilda took a shower, put on a flannel nightdress and went to bed. She fell asleep quickly and dreamed about Richard Calzoni going to jail for defrauding the insurance company.

Harry went to his house and got a pump shotgun from his locked cabinet. He loaded it and put the rest of the shells in his jacket pocket. After making himself a lunch and a thermos of coffee, he parked his cruiser in a driveway behind a hedge, out of sight, but with a good view of Matilda's front door. He tipped his seat back and prepared to wait until the Lincoln showed up. He dozed off and on until his radio brought him wide-awake just before two o'clock. The dispatcher said the turnpike called to say the Lincoln with three tough looking men had passed through five minutes ago. Harry sat up and emptied his thermos into his cup, finding only a swallow left. With the Lincoln at least ninety minutes away, he started his engine and drove to the Quick-Pik convenience store, the only place open all night in town. The man behind the counter said, "Hello, Harry. I just made a fresh pot. Help yourself."

"Hi, Paul. Thanks. I'll fill my thermos."

As Harry got his coffee, he asked, "Did you get your deer, Paul? I know you went out in bow hunting season. Any luck?"

"Naw. I did everything right, but they didn't come close enough. I let an arrow fly at a buck a hundred yards away in the orchard, but it didn't come close. Afterwards, I realized I'd just wound it at that distance and was glad I missed."

"You're right. I didn't get out hunting at all this year. Too busy."

Paul said, "I guess you're always busy. I helped a detective get some clues this fall. I can't talk about it, but she'll let me know when the arrest is made."

Harry's eyes opened as he put the cover on his thermos. He turned around slowly, glanced both ways in the empty store and said, "You can tell me about it, Paul. It may be the same thing I'm investigating."

Paul looked at him and said, quietly, "You know the detective lady that used to work for Doc. She found some clues by the Calzoni's fence. We put them in bags. I can't talk about it, but it may be important."

Harry said, "It is important. I'm working with her. We'll let you know when we find the thief. You've been a great help to us."

"Hey, anytime I can help, just ask. I like to know what's going on around here. I see a lot in this place, some I can't talk about. If I can help, I'll be glad to tell you what happens after midnight in this town. You'd be surprised."

Harry thought for a minute before he said, "There is one thing you can do tonight. I'm expecting some people from away to come into town, three men in a black Lincoln with New Jersey plates. They may be asking how to find Hiram Murphy or Matilda Parker. If so, give them directions to Hiram's cabin. It's at the end of the Picked Mountain road out of Bill's Mills."

"I know the place. The old hermit drove me away when I went up there hunting."

"That's the place. Another thing, even if they don't ask directions, would you call this number and let the barracks know? It is important. Just tell the barracks that the guests have arrived in Lakewood. They'll know what you're talking about."

"Hey, sure, Harry, I'll do that. Just let me know later what this is all about. No, there's no charge for the coffee. Put your wallet away."

Harry drove back to his concealed spot and relaxed with his fresh coffee. He saw a light come on in Matilda's house, then go off again. She was awake. He was relaxing comfortably when the radio blared again. He answered and the dispatcher said, "We got a call from a Paul Bryan. He said you told him to call when the guests arrived. He seemed a little confused, but said they didn't ask for Matilda or Hiram, but wanted directions to the Calzonis. He said we should let you know. Do you know what this is all about?"

"Yes. I have it. Thanks."

Harry was wide-awake. The Calzonis! They were the rich people on the ridge, the ones Paul said Matilda was investigating. Why would the New Jersey men be going there, unless they knew Richard Calzoni? He was generous to all the police and sheriffs in the area. Could he be involved in Hiram's problems? It was time to move. He drove into Matilda's driveway, ran onto the porch, rang the front door bell and saw an upstairs light come on. In half a minute, the porch light came on and Matilda opened the door, looking sleepy, wearing a nightdress, short robe and slippers. When she saw Harry, she opened her eyes wide and blurted, "What are you doing here. It's time for the men from New Jersey to arrive."

Harry said, "I'll come in and explain. Let's get inside."

Matilda held the door and followed Harry into the office asking, "What's going on? Where are they?"

Harry sat in the chair and said, "They've gone to the Calzoni's estate. They got directions from Paul Bryan at the

179

Quick-Pic. They didn't ask for you or Hiram, just the Calzonis. He's involved in this, I don't know how."

"How do you know that? Tell me."

Harry told her about the call from the tollbooth operator, his conversation with Paul Bryan, and the last call from the barracks. The men from New Jersey went directly to the Calzoni estate. It's clear they were expected. Richard Calzoni was part of the problem, and a big part. He must know where Hiram lived. They'd be there by daybreak. They had to let Hiram know.

Matilda called Hiram's number and he answered on the first ring, "Go ahead!"

"Hiram, it's Matilda. The men went to the Calzoni estate. They'll regroup there and probably come at daybreak."

"Are you all right? Did they come see you?"

"No, they stopped at the convenience store down town and got directions to Calzoni's house. Harry is here with me. What should we do now?"

"I've been worried about you. You need to stay with Harry or me. Somehow we've got to keep you safe."

"Okay, for now I'm with Harry. Should we come up to the cabin?"

"No. I can take care of things here. You said they went to Calzoni's place? There are Calzonis in the mob in New Jersey. I thought that name sounded familiar when we started investigating the jewelry theft, but it didn't seem likely some of the New Jersey family would be here in Maine. I didn't tie it together, but if the goons went there, Richard Calzoni must be part of the organization."

"Does that make complications for us? He didn't seem to have anyone around except the Morgans, and they are no threat to anyone."

"It complicates things if Harry has contacted the sheriffs or other police. From what you told me, he has several of them in his pocket. Who else knows they are here to get me?"

Matilda looked at Harry and asked, "Hiram wants to know if you told the sheriff or anyone else about the people coming after him."

Harry said, "No, but that's a good idea. We could use some backup. I can call on the radio and have the barracks alert them."

As Harry stood to go out the door, Matilda said, "Wait. Hiram wants to talk with you."

Harry took the phone and nodded several times and said, "I understand," before he handed it back to Matilda, sat down again and put his head in his hands. The idea of police being paid off to look the other way was beyond his experience. He was aware of Calzoni supporting every police drive for funds, and getting some favors from his boss, but Hiram said he shouldn't call the sheriff or anyone else. The mob had reached Maine.

Matilda talked with Hiram for another few minutes, hung up, sat back in her chair and said, "He wants us to do what we talked about last night. I'm to stay in your cruiser when you park it in the road so they can't get out. They think he doesn't know they're coming after him, and may walk up to the cabin. He thinks he can get them from the cabin, but will need you to come up behind them if they are pinned down. Does that sound all right to you?"

"It's a plan. I hope Calzoni comes with them. The idea of a Mafia boss in Maine sets my teeth on edge. Yeah, I think the ambush Hiram planned will work. I know a place we can wait for their Lincoln to go by headed for Picked Mountain. We'll stay out of sight and let them get up to the cabin. We have time for some breakfast before daylight. I'm hungry."

Matilda scrambled some eggs and made toast. They just started eating when the phone rang. Matilda jumped and answered it. It was Paul Bryan. He said, "That Lincoln just went back by here heading west. I thought you ought to know."

"Thanks Paul, did you see how many men were in it?"

"Not this time. The windows are dark and they didn't stop. You sound upset. I'm off duty in ten minutes. Can I help?"

Matilda thought fast and said, "Do you have your bow and arrows with you?"

"I keep them in my trunk. Why?"

"Do you know the Picked Mountain Road out of Bills Mills?"

"Sure. I've hunted that area."

"Harry Darling and I are headed that way in his cruiser. We'll get there ahead of you, but come up the road until you see the cruiser. I'll be in it. I'll tell you more then."

"Great. This is more detective work. I'll leave here in fifteen minutes and meet you there. Thanks, Matilda."

Matilda didn't stop to get dressed, but pulled her robe tight and got into the cruiser with Harry. He didn't turn on his blue lights, but sped along until he saw a big car in the distance. He slowed down and watched as it turned onto the Picked Mountain Road. He drove by and stopped, waited a minute, then turned around, turned off his headlights and slowly followed the car up the narrow dirt road in the early dawn light. When he saw taillights flash in the distance, he stopped and shut off his engine. He unlatched his revolver in its holster, picked up the shotgun and eased out the door without a sound. He held his hand flat to Matilda, warning her to stay there and be quiet, then slowly started walking up the road toward the cabin. Matilda lowered her window but could hear nothing but the frogs and birds waking up. Then she heard a pounding on the door of the cabin and a hoarse voice saying, "Open up Hiram. We want to talk."

There was a muffled reply, then several gunshots came one on top of another. A man screamed and another yelled, "Angelo's hurt. Get back to the car."

Another shot rang out and another yell rose and faded. Then the rat-tat-tat of a machine gun roared and echoed back off the ledge. The firing continued for nearly a minute, then silence. Matilda waited. All the birds and frogs were silent. Finally the hoarse voice yelled, "You're trapped Hiram. You can't get away. Come out now and we'll take you back to Junior. You don't need to die. Calzoni said it's better if we don't kill you. You've hurt Angelo. We don't want to kill you. Come out now."

The answer was a single shot, followed by a yell and swearing, "You clipped my ear, you bastard. There's no hope now. I thought I put enough holes in you in Trenton. This time you'll look like Swiss cheese."

The machine gun again erupted for half a minute, then silence again. Matilda was straining to hear, when a hand appeared on her windowsill. She recoiled and gasped, then relaxed when she saw Paul standing there smiling. He said,

"I heard all the gunfire. It sounds like a war. I have my bow and arrows. What's happening?"

"Oh, Hi, Paul. I'm glad you're here. The men in the Lincoln are up there, trying to kill Hiram. Harry went up the road. You might go up through the woods, but stay out of sight. They're mean and shooting at everything. I'm here blocking the road so they can't get away."

Paul looked at her for a minute, then stepped into the woods and was out of sight. She looked and listened, but he just disappeared without a sound. It was quiet at the cabin until she heard Harry yell, "Freeze. Drop the gun."

A single shot rang out and Harry yelled, "Shit."

The machine gun again rattled for a minute, then the silence returned. Then there were two shots, a second apart, and another scream. Matilda wanted to run up and see if she could help, but stayed in the car. Another minute of silence was followed by another scream and cursing from the man with the hoarse voice. He said, "Goddam Indians. Where are they? Goddam Indians"

There was another burst of machine gun fire, then a single rifle shot, and the silence returned. Matilda sat with her hand on the door handle, and finally opened the door quietly and stepped out. She looked up and saw Hiram limping down the road, with Paul following him. Hiram said, "Harry's hurt. Come help. We've got to get him to a doctor."

Matilda ran up the hill, passing the two men who turned and followed her. The driveway in front of Hiram's house looked like a war zone. Matilda saw three men lying on the road, then saw Harry sitting on the ground leaning against the Lincoln. She ran up and saw a pool of blood under his leg that he was holding with both hands. She scanned him up and down as she knelt down beside him and asked, "Is your leg the only place you're hurt. Are you shot anywhere else"?

"I don't think so. It's just my leg, but that spurts when I let go."

Matilda took his hand and lifted it to see the wound, and blood spurted up onto her robe. Harry quickly grasped the wound again and said, "We've got to get to Doc."

Matilda glanced around, then started tearing the bottom of her nightgown into strips. She put one strip around the leg above Harry's hands and tied it. Then she said, "Paul. Give me an arrow."

Paul pulled an arrow from his quiver and passed it to her. She slid it under the cloth strip and twisted it around several times until the cloth was tight and the aluminum shaft looked as if it was about to break. She looked at it, and said, "Okay Harry, try releasing the pressure again."

He looked at her in some alarm, but slowly released his grip. There was some ooze but no spurting blood. Matilda took another strip of her skirt and made another tourniquet below the first one and just above the bullet wound. With this tightened with another arrow, all bleeding stopped. She took a clean handkerchief from her pocket, laid it over the wound, and bound it in place with another strip from her nightdress. She leaned back and looked at Harry's face. He was pale, but smiling. She eased him down flat on the ground and said, "You've lost a lot of blood. Stay flat until we get you to the hospital."

"All right. But we've got to get this place secure and a team up here." He looked at Hiram and said, "Call the barracks and tell them an officer is down. Give them the directions and they'll come here."

Hiram ran toward the house as Paul started running down the hill, saying, "I've got to get my car out of the way so an ambulance can get up here."

Matilda looked at Harry and said, "That's right. The road will be blocked with cars. We have to get out of here before everyone comes. Do you think you can get into the back seat of the Lincoln if I help?"

"Sure. My other leg is okay. I'm not dizzy any more."

Matilda opened the back door of the Lincoln and helped Harry crawl to the car. Hiram came back and helped until Harry was lying on his side on the back seat. As he lay there, Matilda looked at his leg and assured herself there was no more bleeding. She got into the drivers seat and turned the big car around. Hiram ran down the hill to the cruiser. As the Lincoln approached, he got out again and shouted, "There are no keys"

Harry said, "They're in my pocket. I can get them. Matilda jumped out and opened the back door. Harry pulled out the keys and passed them to her. She tossed them to Hiram. With Hiram backing up and the Lincoln following closely, they went down the mountain road. They got to the paved road and saw Paul sitting in his car. Hiram backed the cruiser up beside it and Matilda rolled her window down and yelled, "You stay here and tell them what happened. I'm going to take Harry to the hospital."

The Lincoln threw gravel back as she spun onto the road and headed east on the highway. Harry groaned and said, "Not too fast. I'd like to get there in one piece."

Matilda didn't say anything but concentrated on the road and maintained her speed. Halfway to the hospital they met a police cruiser with blue lights and headlights flashing. It didn't stop and Matilda didn't slow down. In less that ten minutes, she skidded to a stop at the ambulance entrance, opened the door and yelled, "I need a stretcher!"

Two nurses helped Matilda get Harry out of the ambulance and onto a stretcher. They wheeled him into the emergency room just as Doc drove in and parked. Matilda called to him and said, "Doc, Harry's been shot. He's in here."

Doc looked at her quizzically as he ran past into the emergency entrance. She started in behind him but a nurse stopped her and said, "We'll take care of him now. You must move your car away from the emergency entrance. Then go to admitting. They'll have some questions for you. We'll let you know when you can see him."

Matilda stood in the doorway, wondering why Doc looked so surprised, then realized that her robe barely covered the bottom of her torn nightdress, and that barely covered her bottom. She walked back to the Lincoln and drove to her office. She couldn't return to Hiram's with the road filled with cars. He could handle the investigation there. She went to her big swivel chair and tipped back, thinking. She remembered the hoarse voice telling Hiram that Calzoni wanted him taken alive. So Richard Calzoni was part of the problem, but the goons were probably all dead. There was no way to tie him to the mob, or was there? She remembered getting his fingerprints to match the ones on the boots. She looked in her notes and found the name of the laboratory used by the insurance company. It was just eight o'clock when she called and got an answering service. She explained that Murphy Investigations had some information about a case under investigation. The operator transferred her to a woman who said, "How can we help Murphy investigations?"

Matilda said, "A week ago we sent some boots and a pocketbook to match fingerprints for an insurance investigation. Do you know if those prints were sent to the FBI for identification?"

"Probably they were, but just as a routine. We had the answer requested of us. We usually do mail them to the FBI. I can check to be sure they were sent."

"Yes please do. It's important to know if they have any record of the man who calls himself Mr. Richard Calzoni."

"Hang on. I'll check the files."

In a less than a minute the woman came back, "They were sent, but without any specific request. I can call and ask them to look at them and see if they have a match."

"Please do. There were several men killed and a policeman injured in Lakewood this morning and I think he may be involved."

"I'll get right on it. I may need to report this to the police. Is that a problem?"

"No. One of the men shot was a Maine State Policeman. He's in the Lakewood hospital now. The police should know if the prints on the boots match a criminal."

"I have your number. I'll call you back in a few minutes."

Matilda again leaned back in her swivel chair, considering what to do next. Assuming Hiram was right, the death of the goons might end his problem, but it might not. Junior, whoever that was, might still want revenge. Calzoni was involved now. The goons were taking orders from him. The State Police Department of Criminal Investigation needed to know what she knew. She called the barracks and asked how to get in touch with Inspector Shirley Nasson, a man she had met before. The dispatcher said he would ask him to call her sometime this week. She told the dispatcher that Sergeant Harry Darling was injured and in the Lakewood emergency room, being treated for a gunshot wound. Suddenly he said, "Shirley Nasson will call you in a few minutes. Stay where you are. I have your number."

Matilda jumped as the phone rang, suddenly realizing how much stress she was feeling. She answered, "Murphy Investigations, Matilda Parker speaking."

"Hello Matilda, this is Shirley Nasson. We need to talk. Tell me what happened."

"Hello Shirley, my partner was attacked by three members of the mafia. Harry Darling tried to stop them. He was shot in the leg. I drove him to the Lakewood hospital."

"Okay, slow down. Is anyone else hurt?"

"I think the three gangsters are dead, but I'm not sure. I put a tourniquet on Harry and rushed him to the hospital. I didn't wait to see if they were dead or alive. The ambulance and another police car are at the scene now. They can tell you."

"Okay, I'll get the reports. I need to talk with you. I can be in Lakewood in an hour. Tell me your address."

Matilda gave him directions and hung up the phone. She started to lean back again when the phone rang. The woman said, "The FBI says the prints match those of a wanted man, Mario Carrillo. They will be in touch with you. They're coming from Portland. I gave them your address and telephone number. They wanted you to stay there and wait for them. Don't do anything else. Mario Carrillo is very dangerous, a killer."

"Okay, thanks. I'll wait here. The State Police investigators are coming to see me, too. I've seen too much killing. Thanks for helping."

Matilda sat back again, wondering why Doc looked at her so strangely, then again remembered her robe was spattered with blood and her nightdress was in tatters. She went to her room, took a quick shower and got dressed. She felt hungry, went into the kitchen, and saw the cold scrambled eggs that she and Harry left when they rushed out. She cleared the table and started a pot of coffee and some toast. She ate four pieces of toast with peanut butter with her hot coffee as she sat thinking about the next step.

CHAPTER TWENTY-THREE

Case Closed

The FBI agents used their four-way-flashers and blinking headlights coming up from Portland, arriving less than an hour after their call. Matilda answered the doorbell and met two young men in suits, both nearly six feet tall with athletic builds. They followed her into the office, looking around every step of the way, seeming to miss nothing. Matilda showed them the chairs and sat behind her desk, waiting for an introduction. One of the men asked, "Where is Mario Carrillo?"

Matilda looked at him questioningly and said, "Hello. I'm Matilda Parker. I think you should identify yourselves."

The men simultaneously reached into their breast pockets and flipped open a leather folder with a badge on one side under gold letters saying FBI, and a photo ID and some writing on the other. They started to put them away when Matilda said, "I need to see them, if you don't mind."

They glanced at each other, hesitated, and then placed them on her desk. She picked up first one, then the other, making notes on her pad of the names and identification numbers. She slid them back to them and said, "It's nice to know who is asking the questions. I've dealt with some unsavory characters today. Now, Agent O'Reilly and Agent Morse, how can I help you?"

Agent Morse asked again, "Where is Mario Carrillo. We need to locate him as soon as possible. He's as slippery as they come, and seems to know what we're doing before we do. Tell us where to find him."

"Okay, he lives on a big estate up on the ridge. He's using the name Richard Calzoni. I can give you directions or show you the way. He has two vicious Doberman pinchers guarding the place. I've been there several times and know the caretaker and his wife. Calzoni, or Carrillo, was home this morning, early, but I don't know if he's still there now."

Agent O'Reilly leaned forward and asked. "You've been in touch with Carrillo today? What for?"

"I didn't say I was in touch with him. I said he was there this morning. The three men who came up from New Jersey to kill Hiram Murphy went to see him about three this morning. He gave them instructions and they wounded a state police officer and tried to kill Hiram."

Agent Morse narrowed his eyes and asked, "How do you know this. We just got the positive ID from Langley this morning. How are you involved?"

Matilda said, "Maybe you need to relax and listen. I'll tell you everything, but we aren't getting very far they way we're going. Can I get you a cup of coffee?"

The men looked at each other and finally sat back in their seats Morse said, "Yes. We could use a cup of coffee. It's not often that one of the 'most wanted' comes to Maine. Sure, we can get the whole story. He doesn't know his cover is blown. We have to wait for our backup anyway. The sheriffs of two counties will be ready when we need them."

Agent O'Reilly looked at Morse and said, "It's interesting. He's using the name of his wife's first husband, Richard Calzoni."

Matilda has started to rise, then sat down again and asked in alarm, "You said you let the sheriffs know you were coming for Mario Carrillo?"

"I'm sure the agency called them. He's a dangerous man and we need all the help we can get. The state police were tied up in another case."

Matilda said, "The state police are tied up on the same case. There isn't time for coffee. He has every sheriff in the area in his pocket. If they know, he knows. You'd better get going now. I'll show you the way."

The two men looked at each other and got to their feet. O'Reilly said, "You can't ride with us, but you can lead the way. Just get out of the way when we get there."

Matilda ran to her Buick and led the agents' car up the ridge road, stopping at the gate to the estate. The gate was closed and a Ford County Sheriff's car was blocking the road. Matilda turned her car around as the agents jumped out of their car and spoke to a burly sheriff who kept his right hand on the pistol in his holster. Matilda couldn't hear what they were saying, but it was obvious the sheriff wasn't going to let them in through the gate. She watched as agent O'Reilly reached for his identification, and the sheriff pulled his pistol half way out of its holster. Matilda realized she wasn't going to be any help and might be in the way. She started back toward town, then got an idea and pulled into the next farmhouse. She knew the woman who lived there and asked to use her phone. She called Hiram and asked if he could come and help her. He said his place was crawling with police and reporters. The road was blocked solid and there was no way he could get down the mountain. Matilda said, "I don't dare to do it myself. Who can I get to help?"

Hiram said, "Do what? I don't know what you have in mind, but Paul Bryan left his car at the foot of the hill. He's still here. I could ask him to run down and come give you a hand. What are you doing?"

"I'll tell you later. Tell Paul to come to where we found the boots, and bring his bow. Tell him to hurry. I'll be waiting there."

"I'll tell him" and Matilda heard Hiram yell, "Paul" as he hung up.

Matilda drove back to the estate. She recognized the Greenville Sheriffs car parked beside the other cars blocking the gate. She drove past the driveway, around the corner and stopped out of sight in the maple grove. She parked her car where Paul could see it and started jogging toward the gate in the fence. If Carrillo or Calzoni, or whoever he was, had to escape and couldn't get out the front gate, he might come up through the orchard and out the little gate that Elmer showed her. She didn't know how she could stop him, but she would try. She stopped running when she could see the gate. She found a rock in a relatively concealed place and sat, catching her breath. The woods were quiet except for a squirrel stirring the leaves in the distance. She sat and watched the orchard through the fence. No one was moving.

After fifteen minutes of patiently waiting, she began to wonder if this was a good idea. Richard was twice her size. There was no way she could fight him. Maybe she could follow him and see where he went, if he came this way. He must have a car hidden somewhere. She could get the plate number and call the state police. But it was dangerous. If he saw her, he might kill her. He had no qualms about sending men to kill Hiram. He might have someone coming here to meet him, or maybe several people. She sat on the rock, questioning her good judgment when she heard a twig crack behind her. Heart jumped into her mouth as she stiffened and turned slowly, then smiled in relief as she saw Paul. He lifted his bow in greeting and silently crept up to her. He said softly, "Hi, Matilda. What clues are we looking for now?"

Matilda glanced at the orchard again and saw nothing moving. Then she said, "The man who lives here is on the FBI most wanted list. He is the one who sent the men to kill Hiram this morning. FBI agents are guarding the front gate and trying to get in, but the sheriffs won't let them in. He may try to come out this way. Do you think we can stop him?"

"I guess we can. I have my hunting arrows with me. I shot the big guy in the leg with a target arrow this morning. He stood up and sprayed with his machine gun, but Hiram nailed him through the head. I've never shot at a person before today. Am I in trouble if I kill this guy?"

"No, I don't think so. The FBI agents said he was wanted dead or alive. If we can take him in alive, that's best, but he's a killer and we shouldn't take chances."

"Okay. Is that the gate over there?"

"Yes. As far as I know, it's the only way out except the front gate."

Paul looked around and said, "I'll need a clear shot. I may get only one. I'm going to find a place about thirty yards from the gate. You may not see me but I'll be there. You can talk to him and get his attention, and I'll shoot if he causes any trouble."

Matilda said, "Thanks, Paul. I'll speak loudly so you'll know what's going on. He has a loud voice, but might be quiet if he's afraid of being followed."

Paul disappeared into the low brush and Matilda was alone again. She felt less alone, but more apprehensive. Now she had to accost him, not just follow him. The doubts returned as she waited, then she saw motion in the orchard. Richard was moving from one tree to the next, always closer to the little gate. He was keeping the trees between him and the front gate, so was easily visible to her. As Matilda watched him come, she slowly stood up and moved behind a bush so she could peek out through the branches. Mario was wearing a bush jacket and tan slacks, as if he was going on a safari. He came to the gate, looked around behind him, then unlocked the padlock. He pulled the gate open and came out, then reached back in and fastened the padlock behind him. He looked through the fence once more, then turned as Matilda shouted, "Hold it right there. Move and I'll shoot."

He stiffened and pulled a revolver from his pocket. He didn't see Matilda until she spoke again, "Drop the pistol or I'll shoot you where you stand."

He looked in her direction and snarled, "Damn you" and raised his pistol. Just as it fired, an arrow hit him high in the back. He shuddered and looked around, then fired another shot in Matilda's direction. A second arrow hit his leg and he fell forward. He tried to roll over but the arrow in his back stopped him. He tried to lift the pistol again as Paul said, "This one in your neck if you don't drop the gun."

Richard turned his head and looked at the broad-tipped arrow six feet from his neck. He dropped the revolver and lay flat on the ground. Paul pulled a length of stout cord from his pocket and tied Mario's hands behind his back. Matilda walked up and stood looking at him, a mountain of a man with an arrow sticking out of his back and another one all the way through his leg. She reached down and picked up his pistol off the ground.

Paul looked at her and asked, "Are you hurt? Did he hit you?"

"No your arrow hit him just as he fired. It scared me. I thought I was going to be killed. I can't stop shaking, but I'm not hurt. What do we do about the arrows. I've never treated anyone with arrows in them."

Paul said, "This one is easy. It has a wooden shaft."

He lifted Mario's leg and took out his hunting knife. He cut off the feather part of the arrow, then jerked it the rest of the way through. Mario screamed and swore, but wasn't able to move. Paul wiggled the arrow in his back, then cut the jacket and shirt to expose the shaft and wound.

Paul said, "I hit his shoulder blade. I really didn't want to kill him. It's not very deep, but it's a broad head on an aluminum shaft and will have to be cut out. I can unscrew the shaft."

Paul pulled on the shaft, twisted, and the arrow came out, without the head attached. There was another scream and Mario tried to roll over. Paul took the pistol from Matilda and said, "A little thirty two, just a pocket pistol. Well, it will make more holes in him if he doesn't behave. I've never killed anyone, but this guy sent the men to kill Hiram. His death won't make anyone cry."

Paul went through the rest of Mario's pockets. There were bundles of $100 bills in several pockets. Except for a penknife, there were no more weapons. Paul and Matilda got Mario to his feet and walked him out of the woods to

Matilda's car. Matilda said, "You are under arrest. I'll take you to the hospital, but you are a prisoner. Do you understand?"

Mario growled, "I understand your life isn't worth a plugged nickel. I haven't done anything wrong. You have no right to hold me. You'll be sued for assault and battery. Just get me to the hospital and get that arrowhead out of my back."

Matilda shuddered a little at the vehemence, hesitated briefly, then looked at Paul and asked, "Can you come to Portland with me? I don't want to take him to Lakewood Hospital. With Harry hurt and the sheriffs in charge, he might get away. In Portland, the FBI and Portland Police can take over. He won't have them paid off."

Mario shouted, "You've got to take me to the nearest hospital. I'm not going to Portland. You can't do that."

Paul pointed the revolver at Mario's head and said, "I think we can. I don't have to work until ten tonight. They said dead or alive. Either way is all right with me. Let's put him in the back seat and strap him in. I'll keep the gun on him while you drive. Let's go to Portland."

The trip was uneventful. The hospital emergency ward clerk called the City Police and the FBI. Matilda insisted that Mario stay in her car until the FBI got there. Police cars surrounded the place when Mario was lifted onto a stretcher and the cords exchanged for handcuffs to the bedrails on both sides. The FBI supervisor talked to the Portland police about keeping him in the highest security cell they had after the surgery was done. Even during the surgery, they were not to let him out of their sight. The FBI supervisor then asked Matilda to come to his office. Matilda and Paul followed him in her car and went into the federal building.

In his office, he was all smiles. He said, "He's been on our most wanted list for four years. He just disappeared. You got his prints and captured him alive. It's hard to believe."

Paul beamed and Matilda said, "It was just part of our investigation. I work for Murphy Investigations. Do we need to make a report?"

"You need to give us your names and addresses. There is a $25,000 reward for information leading to arrest of this man. If anyone ever earned a reward, it's you two."

Paul said, "Wow. $25,000. Matilda, is any of that mine?"

Matilda said, "I think half of it is yours and the other half goes to Murphy Investigations. I couldn't have done it without you. Is that fair?"

"It's great. I wanted to go back to college and now I can. Thanks a lot."

Paul and Matilda talked on the way back to town. Paul had spent two years at the University of Maine studying business administration. After his scholarship and other funds ran out, he started working days as a carpenter's helper and nights in the convenience store, trying to get enough saved for another year of college. The reward money added to what he saved was enough to get his college degree. He told her, "I'll start again in January, unless you want me to keep working with you."

Matilda laughed, "We may work together again some time, but you're better off finishing your education now. You'll be home summers and vacations. Come see me whenever you get back to Lakewood" then more seriously, "You saved my life today, and probably Harry's and Hiram's too. If I can help you in any way, please ask. I owe you more than I can say."

"It was fun. I like working with you. I hope you call me anytime there is anything I can do to help. I may become a detective. What courses do I need for that?"

"To get licensed as a private investigator, you need a degree in criminal justice. I don't know if that's offered at the University. I don't know the curriculum needed. You could ask when you get there."

"I'll do that. I don't think being a businessman is as interesting as being a detective or policeman. If they don't have that course at UMO, I'll look somewhere else. I have a month before the next semester starts. After I graduate, I can work with you."

"We'll have to see about that. Hiram is the boss in Murphy Investigations. I think I could talk him into it, but there's plenty of time to think about that."

They rode back to Paul's car in silence, both deep in thought. They passed a sheriff's car still guarding the gate and the FBI car behind it. After dropping Paul off, she drove back to the gate, stopped behind the cars, got out and walked up to the sheriff's car. The officer stepped out and she said, "Good morning Sheriff Darcy. Aren't you a little out of your territory?"

He squinted and said, "You're the busybody who questioned me about Dr. Price. What are you doing here? No one is going in to see Mr. Calzoni today."

Matilda just smiled at him as the two FBI agents got out of their car and walked up to see what was going on. Agent O'Reilly said, "You shouldn't be here. We're going to make an arrest as soon as this officer gets out of the way."

Matilda smiled broadly, looked from one to the other and said, "If you want to find Richard Calzoni, or Mario

Carrillo, which you say is his real name, you'll have to go to Portland. That's where we took him."

O'Reilly spoke first, "What do you mean, you took him. He's locked in here. He can't get away."

The three men just stood and stared, as Matilda asked pleasantly, "Do you think this is the only way out of the estate? How long did you expect him to stay here, waiting to be arrested? Did he tell you how long to stay, Sheriff Darcy?"

Sheriff Darcy remained quiet but O'Reilly got in her face and said, "Do you know another way out. Tell us now!"

Agent Morse stepped forward put his hand on O'Reilly's shoulder and said softly, "You didn't hear her. She said she took him to Portland. We should hear what she has to say."

Matilda looked at him and said, "Thanks. I'll be glad to tell you about it, but where should I start? Let me say you agents blew it when you called in the sheriffs. Carrillo pays them all off. They do whatever he says."

Sheriff Darcy bristled and said, "That kind of accusation can get you arrested. Mr. Calzoni is an honest citizen. He sues people who defame him. I'll be a good witness."

Matilda wasn't cowed and said, "You are here, out of your county, preventing the FBI from making an arrest of one of the most wanted criminals in the country. I think that would play well in court. Now back off and leave. There's nothing here to guard anymore."

Agent Morse asked again, "Where is Carrillo? Did you say Portland? You said he was here this morning, and the sheriff sure thinks he's still here."

Matilda looked from one of the men to the other as they stood watching her. Finally, she spoke like a teacher talking to children, "Now that I have your attention, I'll tell you. He tried to escape out the gate by the orchard. I was there with a friend. We subdued him and took him to Portland in my car. He's under armed guard in the Maine Medical Center, probably in surgery now getting an arrowhead removed from his back. The FBI supervisor said we would get the reward for finding and capturing him. Are there any questions?"

Agent O'Reilly frowned and said, "How do we know you're telling us the truth? He could still be in there and you're just trying to get us to leave."

Matilda said, "Sheriff Darcy. You have a radio. Have your office call the FBI office in Portland, or the Portland Police, or Maine Medical Center. They'll verify what I said. Agent O'Reilly, perhaps if you turn on your car radio and listen to WPOR, they should have this at the top of their news. In any case, I have work to do. Have a nice day."

Matilda walked to her car as the men started talking to each other. She drove away, feeling good about herself, until she remembered Harry. He was shot and in the hospital. He'd lost a lot of blood and might be near death. She broke the speed limit getting to the Lakewood Hospital. The admitting desk receptionist said he was out of surgery and resting comfortably. She told Matilda the visiting hours were two to four and seven to eight. She was about to argue when Doc saw her and took her by the arm. He led her back to Harry's room as the receptionist glared at them, then shrugged and returned to her papers.

Doc said, "Harry's doing fine. The bullet nicked an artery, but nothing else vital. Your tourniquet stopped the bleeding. I opened the wound, tied off the bleeder and he's stable. I didn't have to give him any blood but he is on antibiotics. He'll be out of here in a day or two, walking with a cane and back to duty in a couple weeks."

They went into Harry's room where he was propped up watching television. He smiled, clicked off the sound, and said, "Hi there. You look fine. Is Hiram okay?"

"He seemed fine when I left. I talked to him on the phone a couple hours ago. He said his place was crawling with police and reporters. He came out of it better than you did."

"Yeah. I thought the man on the ground was dead. I yelled at the man with the submachine gun and he stopped, but the other guy shot me in the leg. I fell and expected another shot, but that was the last thing he did before dying. I was shot by a dead man."

Doc walked to the door, turned and said, "You two can talk, but you stay quiet Harry. That vessel isn't likely to let go, but it has to heal. I'll check back this evening."

"Okay. Thanks Doc."

Matilda looked at Harry. He was pale but in good spirits. She sat down and told him everything she did after she left him at the hospital. When she told him about going to the gate to try to stop Mario, Harry was aghast. "You did what? You thought you could stop one of the FBI's most wanted criminals by talking to him. You're in the wrong business. Now I know why Hiram didn't want you out of our sight."

"It worked. Mario's now in custody and we're getting the reward, or we're sharing it with Paul Bryan. I couldn't have done it without his help."

Matilda answered Harry's questions for the next half hour. When he started glancing at the silent TV, Matilda gave him a kiss and told him she had to go see how Hiram made out. She promised to come back during legal visiting hours. The front desk clerk glared at her again as she left and headed toward Picked Mountain.

The mountain road seemed empty so she started up and made it to Hiram's cabin without any obstruction. He heard her coming and stood in the open door smiling. He called out, "We did it. The bad men are all in body bags and gone to the undertaker. I don't think they'll send anyone else. Your boy with the bow and arrow made the difference. Come in. How is Harry doing? He didn't look bad when he left here."

"Hi Hiram. I just left Harry. Doc patched him up and said he'll be fine. I'm ready for a cup of tea and whatever else you have. I've got some other things to tell you."

Hiram put the teakettle in the sink and turned the water on. He said, "I can make us some burgers if you want. I've got some good lean hamburg."

"That sounds good. Can I talk while you get things put together?"

"Sure, go ahead. Do you plan to talk with Richard Calzoni today?"

"I did that already. He's now in Maine Medical Center in the custody of the FBI. We get a $25,000 reward that I said I'd share with Paul Bryan. He helped me get him tied up and transported to Portland."

Hiram stood with his hand on the faucet and the teakettle running over. His mouth was open and he finally said, "You WHAT? Try saying that in English."

"Okay. Maybe you'd better sit down. I'll start at the beginning."

Hiram turned off the water, put the teakettle on the stove, and sat down looking at Matilda. She explained everything that happened after she left with Harry. When the teakettle started whistling, he ignored it until she stopped talking and pointed to it. He absentmindedly poured the hot water into the ceramic pot while Matilda continued, then sat again. He mumbled to himself but didn't interrupt during her entire recitation. When she was done, he said, "It's a damned wonder you weren't killed. Sometimes ignorance is bliss. I'll have to keep you under my wing if I'm going to keep an apprentice."

"Do you think I need a mother hen to protect me? I'm really capable of looking after myself."

"Sure you are. This time you were lucky. Mario tried to kill you. I don't know how he missed at that range. You aren't bulletproof, you know."

"I'm glad you care. I appreciate your concern, but it's really okay. I've been thinking. It's time for you to show me how to shoot a pistol. I'd have been more comfortable waiting for Mario if I was armed. Can we do that today?"

Hiram shook his head. This woman was going to be the death of him, but then, that wasn't such a bad fate.

THE END

Dewey Richards

ABOUT THE AUTHOR

Dewey Richards grew up on a large dairy farm in rural Farmington, Maine. He had experience as a woodsman, a soldier in the 82nd Airborne, a truck driver, and a pharmaceutical representative before working his way through the University of Maine and Tufts Medical School, selling life insurance and working nights at the Boston City Hospital biochemistry lab. After internship at Maine Medical Center, he established a large rural general practice and became a Board Certified Family Physician, a Maine State Medical Examiner, and an educator. After two years as a Research Associate at Dartmouth Medical School, he spent five years developing and directing the Family Practice Residency at Eastern Maine Medical Center in Bangor. For two years, he was Associate Professor heading the Division of Family Medicine at Tufts, before accepting the position of Professor and Chairman of the Department of Family Medicine at Eastern Virginia Medical School in Norfolk. Dr. Richards finished his medical career by establishing several MedNow urgent care clinics in Maine and Massachusetts. Now retired, he lives in Maine and Florida, enjoying his large family, golf, duplicate bridge, boating, managing his large wood lot in Maine, and writing novels. Visit his web site: www.deweyrichards.com.

Also available is *SOLUTIONS*, a Maine Medical Murder Mystery.

In press is *WIDE SWATH*, a Maine family 1900 to 1950

Printed in the United States
1125100003B/1-69